Book of Never

Spectre

Ashley Capes

Spectre
(Book of Never: 7)
Copyright © 2019 by Ashley Capes

Cover: Illustration by Lin Hsiang, Design by
Vivid Covers
Layout & Typeset: Close-Up Books

ISBN-978-0-6485411-3-4

www.ashleycapes.com

Published by Close-Up Books
Melbourne, Australia

For Brooke

Chapter 1.

Never slipped between broad leaves and approached the first home, its door missing, windows empty and roof near-buried in a riot of leaves; yellows, reds and browns. It could have been beautiful... but his quarry was a little more important than the way in which autumn had transformed the abandoned town into a scene from a tapestry.

He circled the main square, avoiding fallen branches and even a moss-covered bucket as he did so. The next house was just as decrepit as the last, eaves sagging under the weight of time – it seemed the place had been empty for years.

No surprises there. Deep within the forests of Hanik, it'd been hard enough to even find the place at all.

He paused. From ahead, the sound of footsteps crossing barren earth – finally, confirmation. Never drew a knife, hovering over his hand. To draw blood or not? Was crimson-fire really necessary? Maybe not. After all, who else would have come to the ruin?

Never leapt from around the building and into the square, slowing as he saw the figure standing in the centre of blasted earth, dressed in a long, dark cloak of grey.

"Finally," Never said.

The man turned with a smile, his face exceptionally unremarkable. "*Davishca*, this is quite the surprise." He glanced at the blade. "Were you expecting someone else?"

"I suppose I didn't ever tell you my policy on surprises."

"You don't like them."

"Good guess, Cog." Never strode forward, extending his hand. The other man took it. He still wore a scarf at his neck, covering the scarring from his aborted hanging. "I've been searching for you for over a week."

"Then congratulations, that's a swift work," Cog replied.

"Well, turns out I can sense your blood – I felt a trace ever since I returned from Kiymako."

"Ah, I hope it was a fruitful journey?"

Never shrugged – nothing he wanted to go into now, the pain was a little too fresh, even so long after being forced to leave Ayuni. His hand strayed to the necklace her mother had given him; warm, the sense of power deep within. At least Ayuni was safe. Some days the selfish part of him couldn't help but feel such a thing was not truly enough... but it was, if he took a moment to remember the fact. "Somewhat."

"I see."

"Well, you're no doubt curious as to why I've tracked you down."

"I am."

"It's because I need your help," Never said, going on to outline the disturbing things uncovered when he first returned to Hanik and helped Tsolde reclaim her inn – spending significant time on Lord Taginus and his transformation into the brutal creature, and the vibrant red seeds he had devoured to do so. Even now, the blue skin and broken face of bone and teeth... "Have you heard of the Red Seed Cult? We believe they're messing with dark things."

Cog was frowning. "In passing... but wouldn't someone from Vadiya be of more help, Never?"

"Of course – but what I'm really asking is... whether my brother ever mentioned anything about them?"

"No. Mast – that is, Snow did not mention them. I suspect he did not consider them worthy of his notice."

Never folded his arms. Typical, brother. Yet it was bad news, a fruitless search. "Well, they're worth noticing now."

"So what will you do?"

"Return to Lenan, hopefully Elina has arrived by now – I think I need to borrow one of her finest ships."

"Thinking of making an official visit to Vadiya? Risky."

He nodded slowly – and that wasn't just due to the tensions after the war, but Sacha and her promise. "True. Perhaps I'll sneak through the border instead. In which case, I'll make it one of Elina's horses." Depending on the trail, flying was probably a better choice at that. Never glanced around at the town. So little was whole but the sense that it had once been a vibrant place somehow clung to the ruin – he even saw an Amouni rune carved over one of the doorways; *welcome*.

Obviously not a sentiment reserved for Prince Jenisan's father and his men when he came to slaughter the last of the Amouni bloodline. Save for Cog. And Never himself.

"I come here often." Cog pointed to the ruined earth. "Here once stood a well but your brother caused it to erupt with fire. It seared the King's men to nothingness where they had gathered to gloat over the spoils of their secret task."

"Before he saved you?"

"No. I witnessed it," Cog said, his jaw now clenched.

Never put a hand on the man's shoulder. "I am glad he came in time."

"Thank you, *Davishca*. Sometimes I do not know that I agree, any longer."

"No?"

He gestured to the emptiness and Never caught a glimpse of old cloth within one of the buildings. "I had a family here. Friends. People who relied on me. People who brought me joy, Never. It is... difficult to be the last of something, isn't it?"

"Yes."

Cog sighed.

"I know I told you to find your own path, back in the throne room, but you're welcome to join me now. Vadiya isn't too cold in the autumn."

"That is generous... but I do not know if that is where my future lies."

Never nodded. "Duvaya yis je corilu." *I hope the Gods smile upon your next steps.*

Cog blinked, then smiled. "A clever attempt to manipulate me, *Davishca*? These ruins have not heard the Amouni tongue for many years and it is wonderful to hear it now, I will admit."

"Not manipulation I hope... just consider it a reminder that between me, you and my sister, we are no longer the last of anything."

"You are right, of course," Cog said, glancing back to

the homes.

"Well, you know where I'll be heading if you change your mind," Never said as he started back toward the suggestion of a road leading out of town. "Although, I might have lied before."

"How so?"

"Vadiya – it's pretty miserable in autumn too."

Chapter 2.

Never lay across three chairs where he'd arranged them in his room at *The Young Stag*, waiting with both Elina and Luis for Tsolde to join them. The legs scraped on the wooden floor as he shifted.

"That's ridiculous, Never," Elina said.

While it was to be a small meeting to discuss his next move, a part of him had expected Cog to be here for it. Thus far, the man had not appeared.

"I know, but I wanted to stretch out my back and I thought you'd find it rude if I lay on the floor or the bed, while we talked," he replied. "After all, you're the Queen, My Lady." So far, he hadn't had a chance to speak with her but she'd held back her questions about Kiymako and anything else quite well; the Red Seed Cult was no doubt much upon her mind.

"That is actually more distracting, you fool."

Her tone of voice was one of a long-suffering friend, and it was all he could go on to judge if she was truly angry, since from where he lay, all her could see was her crossed legs beneath the table. He glanced up at the ceiling, newly repaired – the scent of sawdust lingering, and quite pleasant.

Far more so than blood and ash that had lingered during his last visit – but any signs of wreckage and the twisted corpse of Lord Taginus were long gone now. Yet the threat of his tainted seeds remained.

"Wouldn't the bed be better?" Luis asked.

"Too soft."

"Is it your wings?"

"Not this time, just my back."

"Getting old, Never?" It sounded as though Luis was grinning.

"Something for you to look forward to."

A door squeaked open. "Never? What are you doing?"

"Stretching – but I'll stop, since it's bothering everyone." He rose with a grunt. Tsolde was taking a seat beside Elina and Luis was pouring water for everyone. Tsolde's curls had been tied into a tail and her hands were covered in flour. An air of contentedness hung around her; helping win her inn back had been worth every cut, scrape and bruise. Elina, by contrast, appeared every bit the queen, a jewelled pendant and pale blue shirt beneath a thick cloak of fine material – the cost of her new position an expression of faint worry.

"So what did Cog have to say?" Tsolde asked.

"Nothing, I'm afraid. I think it's clear I have to travel to Vadiya if we want to get to the bottom of this. Alone," he added.

"Well, there's no-one to send with you," Elina said. "But I want you to know that you have anything you need from me."

"And this is your room as long as you need it," Tsolde said,

Luis nodding beside her.

"Thank you all. I think we'll need to spend a bit of time following whatever trail we can right here. What about Julistya?" he asked Elina.

"She knew little, but supposedly the ship that smuggled her here was one Lord Taginus used, it's the *Swift*. It's not docked here, however."

"I'll search for it in Vadiya. What about the Lord's friends here?"

"Disappeared."

"No doubt heading west." He frowned. "I wanted a little more in the way of a trail here, to be honest – maybe chasing Cog was a mistake."

"Is the trail really that important? I imagine people will know of them, wherever you go in Vadiya," Elina said.

"I suppose so."

Luis put his cup down. "So, will you head overland or go by ship?"

"Overland," Never said. "It's quicker as the Amouni flies, so to speak."

Tsolde rolled her eyes.

"And then what?" Elina asked.

"Look around, see who gets in my way – the usual."

"Wonderful, Never," Elina muttered.

"It's worked before, more or less."

Tsolde stood. "Then I suppose the Stag will be provisioning you – I'll get to work on that."

"Actually, if you could add some writing materials and wax – I think I'm going to have to dust off my forgery skills."

She raised an eyebrow but nodded.

Luis joined her. "Let me start on the rest." He closed the door as he left, and a hush fell across the room.

Never looked to Elina, who had leant back in her chair, expression one of weariness – the lines beneath her eyes a clear sign of the burden of ruling. "You left your guard downstairs?"

"They're quite happy, I'm sure," she said. She met his gaze. "I have been meaning to ask about your sister... Tsolde told me that she lives."

"A prisoner of her role, but yes." He sighed. "But at least I know she is safe."

"She also told me that when you first returned from Kiymako you refused to talk about it."

"That's not precisely true," he said. It was more that, after losing Snow, his only family for so long, to then 'lose' Ayuni to her own fate so soon afterwards... it was not simply cruel – it was barbarism from the Gods. Hard to put a positive spin on that. "But if I'm being honest, I can return and see her any time I wish. It was just... different when I imagined finding her."

Elina nodded, reaching out to take his hand. "I'm sorry, Never." She opened her mouth as if to continue but stopped – and he thought knew why, it was not about Ayuni. The note Elina left, or more precisely, what remained unaddressed in the note. His own confusion had cleared, it seemed, but what was she thinking?

"Something is on your mind," he said.

"Yes." She shook her head. "Before you left for Kiymako... Never, I was wrong to cloud your mind after all that you went through."

He smiled. "You're no cloud, Elina."

She raised an eyebrow, her own smile breaking free. "Still you surprise me; that was almost quite eloquent."

"Good – another feather for my cap; Partial Eloquence."

"I suspect you can guess what I mean to say next, then?"

"That whatever we felt in that moment was nothing to regret but that we doubtless have separate paths to walk?"

She spread her hands with a soft laugh. "That's not so different to what I had in mind, no."

He patter her hand. "Then come and see me off."

"You're leaving today?"

He nodded. "The thing that Taginus became – if there's more of them out there, then I don't want to wait any longer."

Chapter 3.

Flying had not become boring precisely... yet there were little in the way of conversation opportunities when gliding high above the earth. Birds tended to avoid him too. Even they'd be a welcome change from staring at the grey sky before him and forest below, as he bore down on the border between nations, the Folhan Mountains falling behind him now.

So too, his friends had been left behind – Elina to continue working on the possible link between Vadiya agents and merchants, and Luis and Tsolde to keep an eye on the port. They'd sent him off at the edge of town, not overburdened by much in the way of supplies – but enough Hanik treasury money, along with Vadiya shards, to guarantee modest lodgings whenever the chance presented itself.

Which would be Karn; the large town home to one of the biggest border forces in Vadiya, tall and proud upon the plains where it stared across at the Hanik forests. There, he'd as much chance of finding word about the Red Seed Cult as he would in one of the Vadiya ports.

Of perhaps a greater concern was Sacha.

Never banked to chase an updraft. There was no way to know exactly where she'd be or whether they'd even cross paths but the risk was worth whatever trouble would follow – the cult had to be stopped, whatever they were.

Examination of the seeds themselves, which he also carried, bore no fruit. Nor had any of Taginus' gaudy possessions. But something continued to trouble Never – the transformation the Lord had undergone did not have to be linked to the Amouni... but it was still impossible to overlook potential traces of his heritage in any of the more frightful magics that remained in the world. Despite Cog's certainty, there was even a chance that Snow had somehow been involved.

The only way to be sure was to find the cultists in Vadiya.

The *Swift* had supposedly docked along the northern Vadiya coast and accepted goods from overland, perhaps Karn, perhaps elsewhere; either way, the city was still as a good a place as any to begin his search.

Far below, the trees were thinning, groves and stands of woods replacing solid green, the paler plains spreading as he neared the Vadiya border town. Yet well before he came within an arrow's flight from the white walls, Never began to spiral to the earth, descending with the slowly fading sun.

When he thumped down in the swaying grasses a chill had already fallen, as though the very act of crossing the border had invited autumn to pounce upon him. He hid his wings and took a moment to rub at his shoulders and neck before starting toward Karn.

The large town was still some distance away. Small figures moved along the road from the plains; travellers, merchants or farmers, he couldn't tell from so far away but one thing was likely – few, if any, would be from the east.

"Welcome back," he told himself as he started out. Years since he'd set foot on Vadiya soil... back then, it had only been to flee the place.

The grass swished steadily as he walked, and he angled for a trail between fields and quickened his pace through the comparative quiet. Stretching his legs was a welcome change, but he slowed when he finally reached the highway, the sun having already disappeared beyond the horizon and brought dusk to the land.

The white walls of the town stretched up, soldiers walking the parapets, armour gleaming beneath the torches being lit. The people he passed gave him, a foreigner visiting after a war, dark looks but he only grinned at them – winking at a woman who'd offered up a sign to ward off evil, arms crossed and fists closed.

But at the steel gates, which still stood open for now, it wouldn't be enough to simply agitate the locals. So soon after the war, he'd no doubt be questioned or flatly refused by whoever was on duty.

However, they wouldn't be able to refuse him – not while 'acting on orders' from Lord Dakan Isajan, anyway.

Two Steelhawks called as Never approach. Both were heavily armed, from sword to crossbow, and one bore the insignia of a wolf – a senior family. "Halt, *jenaek*."

Never did so, folding his arms. "Watch your tongue, Sergeant."

The man blinked and his fellow put a hand on the hilt

of his weapon. Whether he was surprised by Never's command of Vadiyem or being challenged was unclear. "What did you say?"

"Shut up before I shut you up," Never said, jabbing a finger at the man. "Lord Dakan Isajan is expecting me to make a delivery and if you prevent from completing my task, I will kill you here and dump your head upon your family's doorstep – do you understand?"

The man flinched back, gaping but his fellow raised a hand. "We wouldn't dream of interfering with Lord Isajan but we cannot simply let any pass."

Never withdrew a folded piece of paper with the wax seal of House Isajan, something he'd forged before leaving – and handed it over. "Satisfied?"

The second guard glanced it over, barely reading the words it seemed but instead, focusing on the seal, before waving Never into the town. "Our apologies, sir."

"Forgiven," Never said as he strode inside.

Using Isajan's name was a risk – even considering the long distance between Isajan's holdings and the border, but few in Vadiya would help him – much less consent to speak to him unless he could prove some sort of connection with one of the noble families.

Being the former prisoner of Isajan simply made the man the easiest target for his deception.

And maybe, just maybe, there was a touch of bravado or defiance in the choice too. Something he hadn't admitted to himself when forging the letter, pathetically clear though it seemed now.

"You *want* her to know," he muttered as he strode across the flagstones, heading between broad, low-roofed buildings toward the nearest inn, its door painted with the minimum cost of room and meal, along with a required familial standing. Never frowned. Painting a price was a common enough practice in Vadiya, but the family condition was new. It hardly made sense from a custom standpoint... but in a way, it was no surprise.

Several other buildings that stood nearby seemed to have been transformed into inns, even those which were smaller, suitable for only a few guests. These bore rankings of a generally lower nature. Isajan would have no trouble at any establishment beneath the royal palace itself, and likely the southern family had been invited to the capital in the past too, but the change in custom was still worth some suspicion.

He pushed the door open and entered the Silver Hawk, pausing to scan the common room for a table – only the place was nearly empty.

Three other patrons, all dressed in noble finery of lavender and black sat around a circular table, their three-legged chairs just different enough from Hanik or Marlosa to catch his eye, as they had upon his first visit.

Snow had still been alive then, though at that point they'd long since gone their separate ways. Of course, there was every chance his brother had been somewhere in the southern nation.

"No rooms for *jenaek* here," said a voice from the table. One of the young men sat glaring at Never. He wore a short sword that actually appeared functional. The insignia of a rearing serpent suggested a modest family standing. "Get out," he added in heavily accented Marlosi.

Never shrugged, then paused to make some show of

stretching, even throwing in a yawn.

The angry fellow rose, eyes bulging. His associates did the same, only appearing somewhat less shocked. "Bekarov – maybe he didn't understand?" one of them said to the first.

"No, he heard," Bekarov said as he approached.

Never let the fellow draw close before folding his arms. "Yes, I did hear and let me tell you that I am impressed that a Serpent would disrespect House Isajan so – My Lordship will certainly take note of it when I return south."

Bekarov came to a halt. "What?"

"Come between me and my task and Lord Dakan will ensure your severed head is impaled on a spear and used to sweep out the stables."

The young pup fell back; face draining of colour as he went to one knee. "I have brought shame upon my family."

"You have. Now go, return to them and send offering to My Lord so that he might forgive you."

"Yes, sir."

Never watched the three scramble from the room before he crossed the floor to a table in the corner. He sighed as he sat; the sort of arrogant aggression needed to bully his way in Vadiya was wearying, it had almost been easier as a prisoner.

An older man rose from behind the bar, placing a large box onto the wood. His blonde beard was impressive – it hung over his stomach, braided with black ribbon. "You certainly handled that well."

"Thank you."

"However, I'd like to hear a little more about your lord before I serve you."

Never nodded. Much better. "I could describe the view

of dawn over Siyapol Mountains, how the snow turns to blood, or the way Lord Dakan favours his left leg? Perhaps the way the moat freezes in winter and the children of the keep play a game by sliding pieces of iron?"

The innkeeper inclined his head. "Good enough for me."

"Wonderful," Never said. "Now that that's settled, what do you recommend for someone who has travelled long and far?"

Chapter 4.

Never took a room, though it ate into his silver, and paced the green rug for a time – stopping to take a flask from his pack where it rested on his bed. To do so, he had to reach over a small rail – the Vadiya sleeping arrangements were not unlike cots for infants but the custom seemed to date back to some royal's eccentricity that, for some reason, the populace had sought to emulate.

His next move had to be a little more considered.

Thus far, he'd bullied all who'd challenged him and while it was entirely unremarkable behaviour for a Lord or those in the employ of someone like Isajan, if word spread that Dakan was asking about the Red Seed Cult, there would likely be consequences.

Too long away from Vadiya to know exactly how it would be received.

Would it bring Sacha?

And was that truly what he wanted?

No. Some slinking about the streets or over the rooves would be better. Which meant waiting for darkness before frequenting the dimmer parts of the western quarter, where most of Karn's less honest folk tended to reside. Either that or checking with the priests. He stopped. No, that was a better idea, truly.

Who else would be more aware of a rival religious group?

And in a land with one god and one god only, the cult would be seen as a threat. That is, if they actually held any beliefs and weren't just a front for violence... something he had to confirm one way or another, since it might just make stopping them easier.

He glanced out the window.

Full dark now. Did the Priesthood still welcome the needy after nightfall? Time to find out. Never pulled his hood and strode from his room, heading down the hallway toward the rear exit. He passed a woman dressed in long skirts and a pink shawl, and she flinched from him.

Never didn't bother sighing – he'd experienced far worse as a child, though of course, that hadn't been due to his *Marlosi* blood. Almost refreshing to experience a slightly different prejudice... almost.

Few walked the streets so near the gate. More lights glowed above the buildings further north, nearer the main square before the keep. There, the Winter Defiance Ritual would have most people out, the mass prayer a futile effort to lessen the harshness of the coming winter.

"I don't plan to be here to find out if it will work this year," he muttered as he turned into a thoroughfare, boots smacking on the cold stone. With any luck, he'd find and deal with the Red Seed Cult before winter landed its first strike.

Even so, he pulled his cloak close.

Lamps and torches illuminated enough to lead him eventually to the cathedral, though not without a few detours. It *had* been some years since he'd last set foot in Karn.

But the building was still open at least – wooden doors spread wide and warm light spilling forth, banishing shadow from the short flight of stone steps leading in. The same glow pressed against tall, grated windows; the steel had been forged into the shape of long swords.

Never started up the steps. A priest met him at the top, the young man's bearded face not exactly unwelcoming but nor did he appear remotely close to a smile. He raised a hand, the soft clink of chain mail beneath his white robe clear. "Please state your purpose," he said, speaking Marlosi.

Never answered in Vadiyem. "I have come to request an audience with your High Priest."

The priest frowned. "Foreigners are not permitted to speak with him."

"Then his second perhaps? It is about something that I believe would concern all nations."

"That strikes me as an unlikely claim – if you do not need anything further, I have other duties to attend to." The man turned away.

"The creature I killed bore blue skin, talons and fangs that burst from its face – it had once been a man," he said. "This man ate some red seeds before he changed."

The priest stopped.

"I trust I have your attention now?"

"You do," the fellow said as he turned, expression now troubled. "I will take you to the High Priest at once."

Never followed the young man at a brisk walk through

austere halls, treading upon heavy blue rugs laid on the stone and passing unlit braziers and closed doors, these seeming just as solid, almost militant, as those leading into the cathedral.

A large chamber for worship waited at the end of the hall, though only a single priest stood before a handful of people – most no doubt at the ritual. A large mural of a faceless figure wielding a blazing sword of light covered the back wall; the enemy some manner of dark shape, like some giant cross between dragon and man.

"Minoph, the Servant of God facing down the *Yakeza*," Never's guide said.

Never nodded slowly. That was a little familiar, some of the bedtime stories he'd read to Sacha's nieces and nephews, hadn't they featured Minoph? "I wonder if there are any records of what I have seen held by the Priesthood?"

"I will let High Priest Honislav decide what to share."

"Then the Red Seed Cult is active here, too?"

"For some time. They call themselves the Svikamet – something delusional about a new world," he said. "The first reports of the transformations came from the south-west; they struck while our forces occupied Hanik."

Never missed a step. Hadn't some of the Vadiya soldiers in the Folhan Mountains spoken of the cult? They'd seemed unable to agree on how dangerous the Svikamet really were. Perhaps their spirits had an answer now.

The priest glanced at Never. "I understand you no doubt have less than fond memories of that?"

"Yes, but I'm more concerned with the present."

"As are we here within the Church."

The priest stopped at a set of stairs with a door beside it, the handle of which he twisted then gestured. "Please await the High Priest here." A large table surrounded by chairs waited within, a single lamp burning. Writing materials rested beside it – as though someone had expected to return.

"Thank you," Never said.

He sat and tapped his fingers on the surface. So far, his choice seemed the correct one; the Priesthood was already well aware of the cult. And, depending on how the man in charge reacted, things would be moving quite swiftly. Another good thing, since staying in one place too long was risky.

Footsteps soon echoed down and the priest who had welcomed him led a taller man inside. Like most Vadiya priests, the fellow was part holy-man part warrior – as strongly built as his peers and even armed with a mace, as though he expected attack even within his own stronghold.

Honislav wore a dark beard touched with grey and had shaved his head. He regarded Never with a stern gaze as he sat. "So, stranger. Father Lakiva here assures me you are worth hearing out, so tell me what you have witnessed."

"You can call me Never, High Priest Honislav," Never said. "And thank you for listening."

"Proceed," the man said with a nod.

"The man I killed was not a man when I slew him," Never began, before outlining the events in Tsolde's inn. "I believe he was in contact with merchants from Vadiya for the purpose of smuggling – either illicit goods or people. I was able to save some of the seeds." He withdrew a tiny pouch, opening the drawstring and tipping the two vibrant red seeds onto the table.

Both men gasped.

Never glanced between them. "Something wrong?"

"They are unholy," Father Lakiva said.

"I agree but I don't think we need to fear them – I'm definitely not going to eat any," Never said.

High Priest Honislav folded his arms. "While your story matches many of our own reports and investigations, and the presence of the *disrytha* seed certainly lends credence, I have one concern still."

"Yes?"

The man stood now. "Yes. I wonder why you would lie about your role in the destruction of this Lord Taginus?"

"Lie?"

"It is impossible for one man to single-handedly stop one of the cultists once they've taken the *disrytha*. Entire squads of Steelhawks have been slaughtered by these abominations. Thus, I must conclude that you are lying and I wish to know why."

Chapter 5.

"Two friends helped me – but that isn't the part of the story you need to worry about," Never said. He pointed to the seeds. "It should be the fact that these twisted creatures were born in your homeland, and the fact they threaten all nations."

High Priest Honislav's jaw clenched, causing his beard to quiver. "Heathen! You have no right to lecture me from where you sit upon secrets."

Never stood. "The Svikamet needs to be wiped from the earth – I am offering my help and I had hoped you would do the same."

"Yet you are suspect. Your Vadiyem may be flawless but the only way I would accept that you could face down one of the *stakolin* with only two companions would be if you were one of them yourself. No, it is far more likely that you are in fact a bold but clumsy spy," Honislav said. "The latest of many attempts to infiltrate the Priesthood. And you will be imprisoned here until you reveal all that you know of the cult's nefarious plans. That, my foolish spy, is my concern."

Robust laughter burst from Never. It was perfectly bizarre and yet made perfect sense too – why wouldn't they suspect him? Perhaps subterfuge had been the right choice after all.

Lakiva blinked but the high priest waved an arm. "Chain this imbecile to the dungeon floor."

"No." Never spoke softly now. "I am no spy. And I did kill the creature. I can even prove it to you easily enough but you will not enjoy that. Instead, ask yourself – why would I, a Marlosi man, travel to the land of my supposed enemy after saving people of Hanik?"

"Perhaps that is what makes you an ideal candidate, despite your failure," Honislav replied.

But Lakiva was frowning as he turned to his superior. "Your Eminence, what if he is speaking the truth? Could this be the sign we have prayed for?"

"No, Lakiva. God would not send an outsider to intervene in Vadiya matters."

Never sighed. "Fine, give me a moment and you will see."

With a deep sigh and a frown to go with it, now that they had forced his hand, Never arranged his cloak and let his wings slip free – the black and purple-tinted feathers filling half the chamber, visible at the edges of his vision as he locked gazes with the now gaping high priest.

"You..." he trailed off.

Lakiva seemed robbed of speech altogether.

"Now, believe me when I say I am not a normal man and that I want to stop the cult, and that I can do so."

Still the priests could not speak, and finally Lakiva moved to whisper in Honislav's ear. When he leaned back, the high priest nodded. "You are the Winged Hero of Marlosa."

"If you have to think of me that way, yes."

"Who claims to carry Amouni blood."

"I do not claim it – that is my burden." Never raised a hand to indicate that he was not threatening anyone, then drew a knife from his belt. He cut into his palm, a tiny incision, and summoned a globe of crimson-fire. It tinted their faces. "Let me save your countrymen."

Honislav lowered himself back into his chair. Lakiva sat beside him, moving more swiftly now, his face revealing a deep confusion. The high priest spread his hands. "This... is unprecedented. God, is this your will then?"

Never let the fire wink out and drew his wings closer to his body but did not retract them – better to keep the men off-balance a little longer. "Let me help your people."

"Very well – I will share what we know thus far."

"Thank you."

He nodded though he cleared his throat before speaking, eyes still bearing traces of wariness. "We believe the Svikamet Cult began in Vitrii, beneath the mountains – yet they first harvested their foul seed on the shores of Lake Yusrina. We still do not understand how it came to be, nor why it changes people as it does."

Vitrii – Sacha's home. Was she there? "Have you captured any of them?"

"Of the twelve incidents of *full* transformation we are aware of, all have been killed of a necessity – their rampages become too fierce for anything else."

"Only one has been encountered this far east," Lakiva added. "It may have been Taginus, for we did not see it after Lord Gimaph's men drove it beyond the border."

"Wait," Never said. "You mentioned full transformation?"

"Yes. Sometimes, the cultist is rendered… incomplete by the dark magic. The transformation disfigures and contorts so strongly that they do not survive. In the capital the Holy Father holds the corpse of one such… error," the High Priest said.

"Can we examine it?" Never asked. Had burning Taginus been a mistake? No, it was as the high priest said, a necessity in the moment.

"A request can be made."

"Yusrina isn't so far out of the way if you wanted to see the lake where the seeds were said to be first harvested," Father Lakiva added.

"It probably wouldn't hurt."

"Of those human cultists the Priesthood has captured, few have shared anything of value. We know a stronghold existed somewhere within Mount Siyapol and that they have been sighted much further north too, but little else. Their numbers are perhaps no army but even a single stakolin is an army by itself."

"And their purpose?"

"Mayhem," Honislav said.

"Nothing else?"

"The rantings of some cultists speak of a new society free from the tyranny of a land ruled by kings and priests," Father Lakiva said, his expression now one of distaste. "They refuse to accept the good we do."

Never folded his arms to tap fingers upon his biceps. Finding and breaking the Svikamet stronghold was an obvious task but so was destroying the source of their power; the red seeds. That was perhaps the first mystery – what were they and how did they work? Was there any link to the

Amouni? To Snow's time in Vadiya, unlikely as it seemed? Because if it *could* be traced back to Amouni heritage somehow, as Never was beginning to fear, then it was his responsibility to put a stop to the chaos that was building. "I think cutting off their source of seedlings should be the first task. Uprooting them from their mountain home can follow."

Honislav stroked his beard. "So be it, Amouni. Father Lakiva will guide you to Yusrina, which will allow you to travel unchallenged for the most part. I can arrange for Lord Gimaph to provide Steelhawks too, for if you can truly stop the cult as we have so far failed to do, you must also be protected, Amouni."

"That is generous but I think we will attract less attention as two," Never said.

"Hmmm."

Father Lakiva himself had not reacted outwardly to either suggestion. "Your Eminence, I agree with Amouni Never. You know how large forces of soldiers tend to draw the creatures."

Honislav exhaled. "I do. However, I am reluctant to lose you, who will be my successor one day – neither for a short time as you undertake this holy quest nor if tragedy should befall you."

"I would die in service; that is more than any man should ask."

"But I would ask you live instead and continue your service."

Lakiva bowed his head. "Your Eminence."

"Then we are agreed?" Never asked.

"We are," High Priest Honislav said. "Seek your rest

now and prepare for travel – meet Lakiva here at dawn, for I suspect it is best you leave when fewer eyes are watching."

Chapter 6.

And so he had.

With the sky slowly paling to grey, Never followed Father Lakiva out of the western gate and onto the cold stone of the road. The dark grasses of the surrounding plains stood tall and quiet, doing little to swallow the sound of hoof beats. Never patted the neck of his pale mare; the High Priest had provided them with fine mounts. Glowing pods of light from distant farms spoke of others nearby but at first, they passed no-one on the road, the two exchanging few words.

As the morning grew brighter and warmer, farmers and their carts appeared, headed for market. The priest turned down a narrower road that ran parallel with the western highway.

"Will I draw so much attention?" Never asked. "Surely some outsiders have remained here since before the war."

Lakiva nodded. "Yes, especially further south but I am feeling... concern. Do you know the Echo?"

"Yes. A forbidden art, according to the military and the nobility."

"And the priesthood," he said with a wry smile. "But High Priest Honislav is perhaps more pragmatic than others of his rank; he overlooks my failure."

Never chuckled. "Or maybe more than that – he seems to have rewarded you with a task of great import."

Father Lakiva sighed, glancing to the sky. "So he does."

"Do you doubt yourself?"

"Perhaps. Though I have trained both mind and body my entire life I do not..." he trailed off. "Forgive me, it is not what you wish to hear, you need an ally and that is what you shall have."

"That I can believe," Never said. The Priesthood had long since been forbidden to take part in wars; their remit was Vadiya and Vadiya only, and something strictly enforced by centuries of tradition. And hence the priest's worry – he may not have participated in much more than chasing down criminals in Karn... and what was to come would be a far greater threat indeed. "It has been many years since I last spent time here but the priests I knew in the south spoke of a Holy Thunder – few ever had reason to use it, however. From what I understand of it and from what I faced with the creature, you will be every bit the ally I seek."

Lavika closed his eyes. "Thank you, Amouni."

"Now, tell me about this Echo that has you worried."

"There is something approaching – it may not reach us until tomorrow perhaps, but it is something I have only crossed paths with once. Before the invasion. But it was odd. That is all I can say."

"Time is no concern just yet; we can afford to take slower, quieter paths if you think it best."

"I do."

"Then onward," Never said, tapping his horse's flanks. "When we stop to camp, I can scout around. From which direction do they approach?"

"West."

"Right."

The rest of the morning swept by. Noon too, where they ate in their saddles. It wasn't until dusk that they stopped in a stand of trees set off from the back road. Using such lanes had ensured few people saw them and while Father Lakiva mentioned that the Echo of whatever approached had not turned from its course; it had not made significant ground.

Still, Never took to the darkening skies and circled south then west, leaving the priest to begin their meal. The two tents were small shapes when Never stopped climbing, turning to glide downward, making for the southern limit of the fields broken up by hills and marshland.

While he hadn't travelled to every part of Vadiya, he did recall stories about the marshes beyond Karn as being difficult to traverse. Yet as he neared the wetlands, the fading light colouring the pools and puddles a pale yellow, there was no sign of anything unusual; no large groups, no fell creatures either.

And without knowing exactly what Father Lakiva was sensing Never couldn't offer much, but he was able to confirm that no surprises waited in a fair distance.

He wheeled and started back with a frown. By all the Gods, the wind was too damn cold!

In the camp, now lit by the orange blaze, Never reported from where he almost sat upon the fire, hands wrapped around an empty but still-warm bowl of stew. "There was nothing that caught my eyes and I flew perhaps half the marshland."

Father Lakiva nodded. "That is good, I think. I still cannot discern the purpose of whoever it is that approaches."

"Is the Echo usually so specific?"

"I am not sure. Since it is forbidden, I have spoken to only one other with the ability," he said with a shrug. "But let me watch a little longer tonight, I want to be sure it is no threat."

"Then wake me if you need," Never said as he crawled into his tent. There he removed his boots but little else, pulling the fur blanket close.

Outside, the sound of soft chanting filled the camp; Father Lakiva at work on his prayer. A not unpleasant sound, truly – there was a calming rhythm, nothing that interrupted his rest.

Never closed his eyes.

***

He stretched where he lay, rising to a sitting position before poking his head from the tent. More cold; his breath steamed forth in an unpleasant reminder.

Pale light fell across Father Lakiva, who was already kneeling by the fire, hands upon his knees, speaking softly – another prayer. The fire already burned clean too, a pot boiling atop it. How long had the man been awake? Had he slept at all?

"I trust you got some sleep?" Never asked.

"Plenty," the man said without turning.

"And our visitor?"

"I was not far from waking you – their arrival is imminent."

"Trouble?"

"Now that they are close enough, I sense no ill-will." He glanced over his shoulder. "Rather, it is desperation that I feel, it fills the Echo."

Never pulled his boots on and joined the priest. Faint dust rose along a lane that ran parallel to the highway; someone on horseback then. And it seemed they at least had little trouble locating the camp. Never rested one hand upon the nearest dagger – being prepared couldn't hurt.

"Can you sense anything else?"

Father Lakiva shook his head. "But I know now that they are two."

Never scratched at his unshaven cheek. Two? Who knew he was in Vadiya? It had only been a matter of days and as far as he knew, no-one could communicate the way the monks did in Kiymako.

Sacha.

Yet it could not be, surely. She had no way to know he was in Vadiya.

"Are they seeking you or I?"

"I still cannot tell – it is possible that another with the Echo can find me... but that's not what I sensed before."

"Then this is about me."

"It seems a logical assumption. And we will know soon."

The rider had come into view, still mostly silhouette against the growing light but now the thunder of the hooves reached them.

Closer he drew and it became clear that another figure clung to the pale rider, someone smaller, arms only visible where they held the man. Yet it was the one who gripped the reins that caused Never to draw a breath. A familiar face – one Never had not seen since the war. Not since sending him away. Delicate features yes, but even from a short distance, the man's different coloured eyes, blue and green, seemed to blaze when compared to the translucence of the rest of this face.

Even his hair seemed barely a part of the world.

Andramir.

Chapter 7.

The ghost that was Andramir pulled his horse to a stop and flung himself from the steaming mount – making no sound as he hit the earth. He half-ran, half-glided to Never, expression in turmoil; eyes wide and jaw clenched, blood visible on his lips. Had he bitten it through?

"*Davishca!*"

"Andramir, what's happening?"

"It is Sacha, she has been taken."

Never stiffened – not at all what he'd been expecting. "When? And who?"

"We have been investigating them for some time now. They surprised us weeks ago – we've been travelling for Hanik ever since I failed to take her back. The cost was great, Master, but you are the only one who can save her." The man grimaced and his body flickered.

Never stepped closer. "You're fading."

"I know – such is the imperfect nature of all things."

"But didn't my brother do this? Shouldn't it have been a permanent change?"

Andramir nodded. Tension seemed to be sliding from his body, his shoulders relaxed and his expression became more serene. "Yet I have achieved my purpose – you can save her now. I feared I would not survive long enough to find you but fate has smiled upon me by bringing you to Vadiya instead."

"How can I save her?"

"You are Amouni."

Never reached out to grab the man's shoulders – and his hands found nothing, only slowing, as if passing through water. "That's not an answer..."

"Master, please check upon the boy."

Never glanced to the horse. The second rider lay slumped over the saddle, not so large as a man, clothed in a familiar motley of colours, yellow, red and green – tassels too... Temilo?

Never dashed to the horse and placed a hand on the boy's back. Softly, the expansion and contraction of his torso. The lad was breathing but did not stir. Never glanced over his shoulder. "What hap..."

Andramir was gone.

Faded away to nothing?

"Andramir?" Never waited a moment before sighing. The price of Snow's madness continued. And Andramir had hardly been a hero yet perhaps his final act would prove to be enough for Sacha at least.

"Is the boy well?" Father Lakiva asked as he joined Never. His own face was stoic, as though he had set aside what he'd just witnessed to focus on Temilo.

"Hopefully just exhausted." Never lifted Temilo down and carried him to his tent. There, he arranged the boy, checking on his pulse, examining him a moment. Temilo's features had paled a little; Vadiya was no warm island climate like Ramakki. Worry lines creased his face but at least he was still breathing.

Never returned to the fire, where Father Lakiva was already handing over a cup of the mint-flavoured Vadiya tea. He accepted it with a word of thanks and sipped at it as he stared into the flames. If the Svikamet had Sacha, what sort of chance was there that she lived? And more, would she even want him to seek her?

But that didn't matter for now – she had to be rescued. After that, she could be as angry as she liked.

"I assume the Sacha the strange man spoke of is Lady Sacha Isajan?"

Never nodded.

"I can hardly fathom that she would have such a strange man in her employ."

Never had to shake his head, even as he smiled. "Strange man is an impressive understatement."

"Well, I had no words to describe what I saw. But you knew him."

"Yes... he was once a man but he was changed by Amouni magic. I did not think the change would end up taking his life – I doubt he did either."

"Not the work of God, then." Father Lakiva placed two fists together before his chest and glanced to the sky.

"When Temilo wakes, we'll need to ask him some questions. This might change everything."

"If she is held in the south then I believe you would still find it beneficial to visit the lake, it does not constitute much of a delay."

"I want to hear what Temilo says before I make any decisions."

"It may offer some insight into saving Lady Isajan – and stopping the stakolin if that is still your purpose."

"They are one and the same."

Father Lakiva smiled in what seemed an apology. "I will prepare something hearty for the boy when he wakes."

"I am awake," a new voice answered.

Temilo climbed from the tent, his expression sombre. "Andramir?"

Never shook his head.

The boy – still not quite a young man – looked down. "I see."

"Come, take some food," Never said.

Temilo did so, taking a seat on a log beside Never. "It is good to see you once more."

"And you."

The boy looked to the horse, which was grazing nearby. "I know you'll have questions but I wanted to ask one first. Never? You remember my... debt to Sorga?"

God of Truth. "I do."

"Then tell me, will you do everything you can to save Sacha?" His round face was intent now.

"I will."

The boy exhaled. "I thought so. But I had to ask."

"It's no problem," he said. "What can you tell us? Andramir did not have a chance to share much. We know the cult has her and that you'd been hunting them."

"Yes." Temilo spread his hands. "They can move between places very quickly, with great stamina. It was hard to keep up, hard to predict where they would appear next. They've been killing all over the south. Just not constantly – it's more random. We couldn't figure out why."

"The killing may be its own end."

"It could be. The few we captured... those that hadn't been turned into stakolin, were difficult, even for me to read."

Father Lakiva raised an eyebrow. "For you?"

"Temilo can spot a liar," Never said. "So where were you when she was captured?"

"The Telkash Forests."

West of the marshlands – taking him away from the lake, where the seed may have originated. "What led you there?"

"Andramir was tracking one of the stakolin – it appeared to be heading for the Corpse of Telkash."

"Such a tree truly exists?" Never asked. He'd heard of it but not had the chance to see it – since few prisoners were permitted sight-seeing trips about the country.

"Yes," Father Lakiva said. "I have seen it – the size is startling, were it not a monument to decay I would think it God's work."

"We were attacked before reaching it... half a dozen of them, I don't know. It's all flashes and screams in my memory,"Temilo said softly. He shook his head. "Andramir sent the survivors south to warn Lord Isajan and then we started east, hoping to reach Hanik and you. He called it a slim hope but who else could we turn to?"

Never sighed. "I don't know. But I will find her."

"Do you believe she lives?" Father Lakiva asked.

"All I know is that they did not kill her; they dragged her from the fighting. Others they killed without hesitation,"

Temilo replied.

"That's enough for me," Never said. "And we'll likely learn as much in Telkash than anywhere else – it's a forest, after all."

The priest did not protest, only moving to lift free the pan. "Then let's eat something warm."

"What do you have?" Temilo asked, eyes brightening.

"Nothing fancy but it'll fill you up."

Never let the lad close in on the fire but did not join him. Instead, he started toward Andramir's horse, rubbing the gelding's neck as he stared across the lightening fields.

Chapter 8.

The marshlands stretched on in a grey and green expanse only occasionally broken by a stony hill. A few stands of stunted trees stood here and there too, contrasting with the wide, flat lily pads of a dark green... though Never found himself frowning at them as the road took them deeper. For now, their path was still across stone but at one point, it would not be suitable for wagons – most merchant caravans tended to bypass the place.

"What troubles you?" Father Lakiva asked.

"Isn't it too cold here for lily pads?" He pointed a nearby pool, where half a dozen of the great pads lurked, their flowers sitting like pale, spiked stars of yellow.

The priest nodded. "For true lily pads yes – those are traps set by the *losakegn*."

"Not a creature that appears much in the south, I take it."

"Think of it like a large frog covered in weeds and other plant life – they prey on insects and small animals, mostly. Sometimes birds."

"Andramir said they only live here," Temilo said, his voice still heavy with sadness. "I saw one drag a mouse under, on our journey."

"Then I'll stay right up here then," Never said. He tried to put a little extra levity into his voice but the words rang a little hollow.

Temilo had fallen into silence and Father Lakiva was equally reticent. There was much Never wanted to ask Temilo about his time with Sacha and Andramir but it didn't seem to be the right moment. And so their ride remained quiet as the day stretched on. A quick stop at noon on an uneven clearing to eat and drink from their water flasks and then it was further west.

Late afternoon brought some change to the marsh; yellow and green vines climbed the trees and covered the ground near the water's edge, and the path had grown thinner now, even the stones had started to sink. Some parts of the road were now hard-packed earth and other areas rested beneath a thin layer of water.

"How much worse does it get?" Never asked. His mount's hooves splashed water, scattering hovering insects.

"There are places where the fourth king of Vadiya had to sink great slabs of stone to ensure a passage but we will not have to swim," Father Lakiva said.

Never glanced to the sky. The sun had not yet begun its true descent but it was sinking toward the horizon where, farther on, the forest waited. "Are there regular camp sites?"

"We should reach the Centre Refuge just after dark."

"That sounds official."

"It's something of a walled enclosure – it has simple shelters, stables but nothing like an inn."

"The Refuge was empty when we used it before," Temilo added.

"And is that usual?"

"The paths around the marsh are more popular," Father Lakiva said. "Though not so direct. Depending on the time of year, bypassing this place is actually quicker."

"Well, it sounds warmer than sleeping out here," Never said. "And at least more defensible if we're attacked."

"By who?"

Never shrugged. "I have no idea but I prefer to be the one delivering surprises rather than receiving them."

"I doubt the stakolin followed us," Temilo said.

"I look forward to learning that you are correct," Never said.

And he was. Or so it seemed, since they found only one other traveller within the Refuge – a merchant whose mount was laden with bolts of cloth, each wrapped in oiled coverings. The man sat at his own fire before the shelter, little more than a three-walled enclosure with mud and thatch roofing. And while the fellow responded to the greeting Never offered, he did not seek to join them at their own fire.

Some news of the west would have been welcome but once more, the man proved difficult to engage – seeking his rest before Never had even finished his meal. "It seems needlessly cruel to wake him," Never mused.

"I feel nothing untoward via my... senses," Father Lakiva said.

"Good. And I'll scout the marsh again tomorrow," Never added. "Which means we can get some rest now."

"Will we post a watch?" Temilo asked.

"Wake me for the middle watch," Never said as he sought his blankets. "I'm inclined to believe we are safe here... but I don't think it will hurt to take a little care."

Never stretched out and found sleep came quickly – though he was being woken by Temilo almost right after, or so it seemed. Still, he replaced his boots and drew his cloak near as he moved to a position nearby where he could watch both the wooden gate and the merchant's shelter, both lit by the pale moon.

Yet neither offered movement.

He walked the length of the enclosure, crossing hard dirt and new weeds alike, slowing when he reached the opposite fence. Something seemed amiss. Yet what? The wooden fence was just taller than Never, lashed together with rope and chinked with mud – sturdy, no gaps or holes.

No intruders.

Was it beyond? Never unfurled his cloak, flipping it back from his shoulders and let his wings free. Then, he launched himself into the air, landing softly on the wall. There he perched, peering into the shadows beyond. The marsh appeared empty – moonlight brightened the water but heightened the shadows of hills, trees and depressions. Not a trace of movement beyond either, but someone or *something* lurked there.

He glared into the night.

The sense of being watched did not fade but nor did it intensify to anything more. Whatever was out there did not seem to be close to attacking – if that was its purpose. But could he trust the feeling? Nothing to suggest *how* he knew there was no immediate threat.

Or was whatever waited out there so strong that even its watching was enough to alert anyone who was paying attention?

Yet nothing changed in the marsh during his watch. When he woke Father Lakiva and warned him, the man gave a solemn nod. "God will watch over us, rest easy."

"So long as you watch too, Father," Never replied.

"I will, though I am surprised to note you seem to carry so little faith."

"You are?"

"Of course. The Amouni were said to have been placed between God and mortal man. You were humanity's link; surely your belief in them is firm."

Never smiled. "Perhaps too long a conversation for this night."

"I understand."

"Wake me if anything happens."

"I will."

Once again Never sought sleep though it remained fitful – still, when he woke to the sounds of a risen camp, a restless energy came with him. Father Lakiva and Temilo were talking over the fire, faces shadowed in the grey light. The merchant was gone, his shelter empty.

"I'm going to check the area," Never said when he joined the others.

"Father Lakiva told me you sensed something last night," Temilo said.

"Yes. We were being watched... I don't feel it now but that doesn't mean much. If you break camp, don't wait for me – I'll find you."

With that he strode into the open and once again freed his feathers before taking a running leap, beating his wings to climb up and over the wall. The air was still cold so early in the morning; it widened his eyes and banished the last vestiges of sleep. *Likely for the best.*

Once aloft, he wheeled to glide over the area where he thought the watcher had lurked, holding steady long enough to spot a patch of crushed grass in a small stand... dark stains covering the ground beside something pale.

Nothing appeared out of place nearby; just damp earth, dark pools and empty animal trails. He descended, fanning his wings and touching down to examine the earth. Large footprints covered the space, earth and grass torn as if by claws but there did not seem to be multiple tracks in and out of the stand, just one set heading deeper into the marsh; wide-spaced as though great leaps were taken.

Had it lain in wait for most or all of Never's watch?

The smell of dirt in the hiding place was strong but it mixed with another scent – blood.

Blood covered the grass too, centred around a pile of animal skulls and other bones. Mostly those of small creatures but a few fish too... and all were a bright white, as though they'd been licked clean.

And so many of them.

Almost as though it came willing but also *prepared* to wait?

As though it had brought along food to eat while it watched the walls.

Chapter 9.

Finally the marsh lay behind them.

Never glanced over his shoulder once, letting his horse lead, and the marsh burned gold beneath the rising sun. For now, no-one appeared to be trailing them.

After returning from the creature's vantage point, Never had followed Father Lakiva deeper through the marshlands for two more days before they broke from the dampness, crossing bridges and giant stone slabs lain close together, making fair time but coming no closer to understanding what had been found.

"That doesn't match the behaviour of those we've encountered," Temilo said. "Lady Sacha thought the stakolin became more like animals than human, that bloodlust took over... we saw it more than once."

"That doesn't sound like a creature able to wait and watch, does it?" Father Lakiva said.

"No." Never rested both hands on the pommel of his saddle. What did that mean for Sacha? For Vadiya? For all the lands? If the stakolin were being created in any significant number... "How long until we reach Telkash?"

"Before noon. We'll pass through Pekonuv before then. It might be worth expanding our supplies there," the priest replied.

"Sounds good to me."

They rode at a canter now, the road solid stone once more, the plains spreading in long, broad depressions and once over a modest bridge that spanned a thin river. Still, few farms were visible until mid-morning – yet after cresting a small rise, Never slowed then reined in his horse.

Figures filled the road, travelling in small groups or alone, many burdened by large packs, often blankets sewn together. One group seemed to be pulling a wagon; it, too, piled high with belongings. The nearest was nearly within earshot, and Never hailed the man with a wave.

An older fellow, he was striding with only a thin bag upon his back. "Turn back, Father," he told the priest when he drew close enough. "A beast is loose and not even a man of God can stand before it."

"What do you mean?" Father Lakiva asked.

"The stakolin – like has been seen in the south. We're leaving."

"For where?"

"Some went west to the coast. Many of us are travelling for Karn," he said as he continued.

Never turned his mount. "Is Pekonuv safe?"

"No longer, stranger."

More people were passing now, expressions harried. Few would stop to speak and none would discuss what happened in the town – though one of those who sought comfort from Father Lakiva mentioned the inn.

"We did not see it," one woman said, sword belted at her waist. "It came in the night and when we woke..." she shook her head, hands trembling. "Find another path, won't you?"

When the flow of people had eased, Never exhaled. "I think we have to ask whether something else is happening here."

"What do you mean?" Temilo asked. "Do you suspect some new creature? We don't know what happened yet."

"No... but once again, sneaking around town at night and doing something that terrifies the townsfolk, still doesn't sound like bloodlust."

"It's the human cultists," Father Lakiva said, snapping his fingers.

Never nodded. "That seems likely."

"That makes sense," Temilo said. "But I hope I haven't misled you both. Once they change, they're not purely animal – they're still intelligent, especially before they kill."

"What else do you know of them?" Never asked.

"The first one we found... it was giving orders to the regular cult members, like strategy. Once My Lady and her Hawks engaged however, and the thing tasted blood, then it seemed to lose control."

"Then whoever ate those animals and watched us, had remarkable restraint – or only human blood triggers the bloodlust," Father Lakiva said.

"Or some can calm themselves better, or regular cultists are eating the animals as part of some ritual, we can't know yet. I suppose we're just guessing until we know better," Never added. "But I don't want to overlook the possibility that it's a larger force, rather than a single creature out there."

"Wise words," Father Lakiva said.

"Let's see what waits in Pekonuv then," Never said as he tapped the flanks of his horse.

This time, he didn't slow for the few remaining travellers on the road, instead continuing on until the first homes of Pekonuv appeared. Stone buildings arranged along dirt streets, most with thatch roofing, the only one with stone being a two-storey structure – doubtless the inn.

"Stay together," Never said.

The hooves echoed in the hush. No residents, if any remained, peered from behind doors or windows, their gardens of lavender empty, chimneys cold.

"Is no-one here now?" Temilo asked.

"Seems not." Father Lakiva held his war hammer in both hands, steering with his knees as his gaze moved across the village.

Never hadn't drawn blood yet but he, too, kept a hand near a blade but in a small square before the inn, he let it fall to his side as Father Lakiva gasped.

A scarecrow had been erected before the inn's doors.

Made from entrails, it gleamed in the mid-morning sun, blues and reds vivid against the grey stone of the building. At first glance, Never could not tell just how many or whether from animal or man but they were wound like rope around to form a thick, truly man-like shape. Yet, as though the entrails were not enough, the head was a pumpkin carved in Vadiya script – and he recognised enough to know they were names.

"There are so many," Father Lakiva breathed as he slid from his horse and ran forward. "It is every name... every one of them."

"Who?" Never asked.

"The townsfolk. I recognise enough," he called.

"Why aren't there any birds?" Temilo asked, his voice soft, tone one of shock.

"Don't lose your head," Never told the priest. "This could be a trap."

"For who?" Father Lakiva asked as he spun. Tears ran down his cheeks and his knuckles were white around his hammer. "Who knows we come this way? Who knows you are even here?"

"Whoever was watching last night," Never said as he wheeled his mount – but their back trail stood empty.

Chapter 10.

"I will bury it," Father Lakiva said.

"We can help," Never offered.

He shook his head, eyes red from weeping. "Thank you but it is my burden as their priest. God will lend me strength."

"Then we'll prepare a meal inside," Temilo said, his voice soft.

Never accompanied the boy into the inn's common room. Empty tables and an empty stage, small twin boxes nudged to the side where children played guessing games. Only now, no sounds of sliding wood on wood or squeals of laughter.

The bar was empty, so too the kitchen; stove cold and larder empty.

"I'll start sorting things here," Temilo said, hefting his pack onto one of the tables. "Even if there's not much left, there's a lot of cooking implements."

"No need to get too carried away – we won't be staying here overnight."

Temilo nodded. "I suppose not... but cooking will ease my mind a bit."

"Then keep an ear on the sound of Father Lakiva's shovel."

"Where will you be?"

"Once I finish searching the inn, I want to scout the area again." He paused. "The stakolin are no match for Amouni, Temilo."

The lad sighed, nodding to himself, seeming to take heart from Never's claim.

Nothing was amiss upstairs, simply more empty rooms, most beds made but a few with blankets simply cast aside. The stable was equally vacant, though from the amount of feed left a few horses had once been housed in the inn's stable yard. Perhaps those had travelled west toward Olia.

As he had so many times of late, Never let his wings free and took to the skies. He circled the town but found no sign of any cultists and the small shapes of those nearest were still fleeing Pekonuv.

So what was the true purpose of the scarecrow?

To instil terror? To empty the town? It was becoming less likely the grotesque creation was a trap. No-one had appeared, and as Father Lakiva said, who even knew Never had travelled to Vadiya?

No, the more likely target was the priest himself; he was a threat to the cult.

Temilo too. Perhaps the Svikamet believed Andramir and the lad had learnt something.

Never glided back down to the earth and returned to the inn, then the kitchen.

Lakiva had joined Temilo now, they sat in silence, eating bread while eggs fried in the pan. When the priest spoke, his voice was a little hoarse. "I suspect they were mostly animal… but some seemed to be human. I did not perform full rites as I should have. It may not be safe here."

"Agreed," Never said as he accepted a hunk of warm bread from Temilo and took a bite; the warmth more inspiring than the flavour. "We could travel on but I wonder if we shouldn't slow from this point."

"Why?" Temilo asked. "We need to save Lady Sacha."

"I know. But we're being watched and I'm beginning to think someone in the cult is either toying with us or targeting either of you two. Father Lakiva because of his role and you Temilo, in case you know something."

"If I did, wouldn't they have taken me too?"

"From what you told us, it didn't seem they tried?" Never asked.

"Andramir always kept me away from most of the fighting."

"No," Father Lakiva said. "Your first deduction is correct, it is about fear. They are trying to spread terror and undermine the people's faith. Whatever they try next, here in the north, will be followed by claims that God has abandoned the people for failing to save them."

"As they have tried in the south?" Never asked.

"Supposedly it is working in the city slums but also in the more isolated areas, according to the High Priests."

"Then we stop them here in the north and find Sacha at the same time," Never said. "We can prepare here then head for the forest."

"How can we prepare?" Temilo asked.

"By going over every detail Sacha and the Priesthood uncovered – tell me everything, no matter how inconsequential it may seem."

"It might not be much," Lakiva said.

"Let's lay it all out first," Never replied. "Then I can decide how much I'll need to improvise."

"And you've had a lot of luck with that in the past?" the priest asked.

"Well, I'm still alive, aren't I?"

***

After half a day travelling within the forest, Never decided the Telkash seemed an uncertain place. It matched his mood, for little had come from their pooling of knowledge – the stakolin were still largely unfathomable.

Above, some green clung to the leaves in random groves throughout the stretching woods but more were brown and yellow, and just as many seemed empty already. Light was dim due to the overcast sky but instead of rain, raven calls filtered down from the branches. Loam covered the road, muffling the horses. Grey lizards with dusky orange strips darted about the undergrowth, the first few catching his eye. Most were big enough to rend flesh with their claws but they kept their distance.

"We did not venture very far within before being attacked," Temilo said. His eyes roved as he spoke. "They drove us deeper and we took the left fork up ahead."

A ring of larger elms surrounded a log bridge that led over a rocky creek. Beside it, a winding trail branched off to climb alongside the waterway.

"Do you sense anything, Father?" Never asked. For his own part, the feeling of being watched had not returned.

"Nothing. There is a bear much higher up. She must be close to hibernation but nothing else."

"Keep a watch on her too, if you don't mind," Never said.

The trail wound up and through the tall, rough trunks. Here, the scent of the forest grew duller with cold, even as the sound of the creek rushing downhill grew stronger. But it was a short climb and when he crested the rise, a wide plateau was revealed; trees ringing it but thinning out the closer they drew to the centre, where a giant stump reared toward the open canopy.

It was a cathedral of jagged brown peaks; tall as the walls of a city. Dark holes and rents covered the surface, stunted branches jutting forth. A gaping maw waited at the stump's base – the breadth of the trunk so wide as to rival the massive gates of Isacina. Whenever it had lived, the tree must have been a mighty giant.

Corpse of Telkash.

Yet the wreckage of its trunk or canopy did not surround it.

Instead, armoured bodies covered the ground. The corpses of horses too, flies crawling, all covered in a light sheet of brown leaves, softening the clumps of death. The trail of dead led close to the trunk's maw, where light fell within.

"They struck as we neared the trunk," Temilo said.

"It didn't start further back? They waited for open ground?" Never asked.

"Yes. At first we held our own; it was mostly human cultists but once the first few stakolin joined the fray it was too much," Temilo said, eyes locked to the massacre.

"And where did they take her?"

Temilo pointed further west. "She was screaming for us to fall back – the biggest one struck her on the head with a branch." The boy swallowed. "It seemed like she was alive after that... I think."

Never put a hand on his shoulder. "You couldn't have done anything, and if you'd stayed and died, I might not have known any of this."

Temilo's nod was Never's only answer.

"There is something within the hollow," Father Lakiva said.

Never led them closer, passing the dead, many torn and bloodied beneath dented armour. Still-visible drag-marks nearby suggested someone had taken their fallen. The Svikamet?

"They will all need to be buried when we're done," Father Lakiva said.

"Let's see what we find here first," Never replied as he dismounted before the giant trunk. Up close, black beetles slipped into the cracks within the tree, but theirs were insignificant movements – he stared into the hollow where light fell upon a sword.

It had been driven into a mound of earth; blade almost gleaming in the pale light that streamed in from above.

Words had been seared into the blade, running down toward where the tip had been sheathed, but he could read the first few easily enough – *Lady Isajan*. Bastards. Parting with her blade would have been a torment if she'd been conscious for the moment.

Never climbed the small mound with clenched teeth, ripping the blade free. The red talon of House Isajan was raised beneath his palm, the maroon jewel in the pommel unbroken.

He rested the longsword across both hands and read

aloud. "Bring the Amouni to Mount Syapol if you want to see Lady Isajan again."

Chapter 11.

Sacha's sword hung heavy at Never's side as he followed the cult's trail beneath darkening skies, the forest closing in around them. There was a chance she was alive... they needed her. House Isajan was powerful in the south, perhaps it was military information they sought, perhaps a letter of ransom had already been sent to her father but one purpose was extraordinarily clear.

She was bait.

"For me," he whispered.

What did the cult seek? His blood seemed the most obvious desire. The purpose was more oblique. It probably wasn't to extend lifespans, to recapture youth, how it had been for Hiruso in Kiymako. After all, part of the accelerated power of Ayuni's blood came from her lineage as Phoenix. And there was no link between the cult and the islands either – the Svikamet would have no knowledge there to draw on.

Did that suggest something about the seeds themselves? Was the blood going to be fertiliser to create more powerful creatures? *That* was a troubling thought. Chasing Sacha to the mountains, whether she was alive or not, was akin to delivering himself into their hands.

And going in unprepared would be foolish in the extreme.

Perhaps no more foolish than charging to the aid of a woman who'd promised to kill him...

He needed more information. Not just about the cult, but their design – he needed to place himself a few steps ahead of their plans. And maybe even a few steps ahead of them in the literal sense too. After all, they had a head start of days already...

"I need a river," Never said as he straightened.

"Why? We have plenty of water," Father Lakiva said.

"No, something more than the creek. Something deeper – we need to get ahead of them and set up an ambush of our own," Never said.

"You want a boat?" Temilo asked.

"I have something faster than that – and it's not flying along the river course, in case you were going to suggest that."

"Amouni magic?" he asked.

"Yes. Who has the map?"

Father Lakiva pulled his horse alongside Never and rummaged through one of his saddlebags before bringing out the scroll. He unrolled it and pointed. "There, the Kraidav. It is a strong river. We would reach it early tomorrow if we rode through the night."

Never rubbed at his neck. "What I have in mind won't require that – we can get a real jump on them if it succeeds so we can afford a good rest tonight."

"Can you explain it to us?" Temilo asked.

"It's easier to show you when we get there, actually," Never replied.

***

Rain had started to fall by the time they found a hollow suitable for their mounts and the three tents. It was not strong enough to stop the fire – though it hissed – but it chilled the air and Never found himself frowning around his meal.

"Missing the sun, I take it?" Father Lakiva asked.

"Very much."

"Well, now is as good a time as any for you to share what you have in mind."

"True." Never set his food aside a moment. "Here is what I propose. We know they are heading back to their mountain stronghold, so all we need to do is get ahead and set up an ambush in a suitable location. We track their approach via your Echo and hit hard and fast."

"A sound enough tactic but there are many unknowns – their path for one. If we arrange some manner of ambush and the cult takes another road?"

"If we get close enough you should be able to feel them?"

"It's likely, yes."

"The creatures we tracked had endurance like horses," Temilo said. "Can we really get ahead of them?"

"Their human counterparts won't be so strong, I imagine," Never said. "But if we use that as a marker anyway, and assume they're taking the most direct route to the mountains at significant speed, they still can't have reached Yusrina yet."

"So you'd bring a force from the city?" Father Lakiva asked.

"Perhaps."

"And then what?"

Never glanced into the flames. The road leading to Yusrina passed through a series of canyons and a bridge... what was it called? The Tsaga-something-Bridge. Det? No, *Dek*. "The Tsagadek Bridge."

"That might have possibilities."

"Are you sure we can afford to stop now?" Temilo asked. "And you still haven't answered *how*, Never."

"We can stop – and nothing is faster than the rivers," Never replied. "Tomorrow I can show you, so rest easy tonight."

***

The Kraidav River swept between the tree trunks like a dark serpent, deep but not particularly wide. Fallen leaves gathered at the edges or flew with the current. Never paused at the edge, careful with his footing, since the banks were half-buried in fallen leaves and all remained slick from last night's rain – especially with the morning sun still fighting its way free of the canopy.

"Before I call, I want to warn you – it will be a swift passage through darkness and coloured lights," Never told the others. "I doubt the horses will be able to follow, so we should take what we can carry."

Father Lakiva hesitated before nodding. "I suppose we can find new mounts in Yusrina."

"Will it hurt?" Temilo asked.

"No – in fact, you'll be dry when we're done," Never said with a smile, then he turned back to the water. He raised his voice, calling in the Amouni tongue. "Guide."

The water stirred as a figure began to rise, the silver scales of a fish head and then a woman's bare shoulders, her robe of lilac – save for a portion near the bottom, it was a golden colour. Yet it was not two pieces of cloth or two colours... it was *two Guides*. As if they had been sewn together with invisible stitching. How could something even be attempted? And what did it mean – was it more of Snow's work?

Twin gasps rose from behind Never.

Master.

"Guide, are you whole?"

Of course.

He frowned. "Truly?"

Yes. You have restored me. For that, I thank you.

Almost definitely Snow's work then – and his brother had hardly been one to undertake poor craftsmanship; the Guide would not fail. "Guide, we must travel to Tsagadek River – on Yusrina's bank."

So it shall be.

Never motioned for the others to come closer. "Temilo – take my hand and do not let go, no matter what happens. Father Lakiva, you take his."

Temilo gripped hard, eyes wide and the priest took the boy's other hand, murmuring what was most likely a prayer. Never stepped into the river and caught the Guide's outstretched hand, the chill water washing over him only for darkness to envelop him a moment later.

The cold vanished.

Light blazed in purple and blue as it streaked by.

Temilo's grip tightened yet further, the lad was certainly entitled to whatever he was feeling.

Time did not seem to pass slowly nor especially quickly and before too long the Guide was speaking once more. Never still couldn't judge the time span.

We have reached the banks of the Tsagadek, Master.

"Thank you, Guide."

Growing light revealed a cloud-strewn sky and lush grass along the bank of a churning river, jagged rocks visible where the watercourse dropped in a series of steep cliffs. Tsagadek Bridge itself loomed nearby; an arch of pale stone with dark railings and twin guard posts in not only the nearest bank but in the middle and the far side too.

A shout rose from nearby.

Never spun. A band of soldiers, regular infantry, were scrambling back from where they had stopped to take water. One fellow stumbled into a companion, tripping himself. "They just appeared from the water!"

Another man frowned. "How did..."

"Forget what you have seen, my son," Father Lakiva said. "Go on your way calm in the knowledge that we are not bringing harm to any."

His words seemed to bear an additional resonance... something beyond what was human, and they were soothing too, commanding perhaps as a parent who knew best.

Together, with some muttering and a few glances, the group gathered themselves and started for the nearby road. Once they reached it, their footfalls echoed toward the city, whose not-too-distant walls rose from the plain. Black flags hung limp from the towers, the spear-like palace matching with its black and deep-blue tiles. The pattern, not so clear from their position, was a coiled water serpent.

"I'm completely dry?" Temilo said, wonder in his voice.

"See?" Never grinned. He turned to the city. "Father, will the priesthood help convince the Lord to supply us with men for our ambush?"

"If we can prove they are due to take this path."

"It will be at night, I imagine."

"So what if they don't take the bridge?" Temilo asked.

"Isn't the nearest alternative to travel east around the lake? It's a considerable delay." Never turned to the priest. "What of your Echo, do you sense—"

"By God, they are coming now!" Father Lakiva cried. He charged for the bridge, war hammer in hand.

Chapter 12.

Never dashed after the man, skidding to a halt on the worn stones of the bridge. He shielded his eyes, but saw no-one crossing, nor approaching from the dark trees beyond the span. Water rushed some distance below, causing him to raise his voice. "Where?"

"They'll be upon us before noon – the Echo is building, there are at least two of the stakolin and half a dozen cultists."

"And Sacha?" Temilo asked.

"I cannot tell one way or another," Father Lakiva replied. His brows were drawn together as he stared across the bridge.

Never glanced up at the sky; the sun would reach its zenith soon, far too soon to reach the city and return with a force of any size. How did the cult travel so swiftly? It shouldn't have been possible. Gods damn them!

"Never, what do we do?" Temilo asked. "You're going to save her, right?"

"I am," he said. He knelt before Temilo. "But I need you to stay out of the fighting."

"I want to help—"

"I know. The best way is to warn the city, can you catch up to those travellers?"

He nodded but his expression was one of frustration.

"Good. Now go; and do what you must to convince them. We need Steelhawks and priests."

"Right." The boy sprinted after the travellers.

Never turned back to the bridge, pale and empty. "How long now?"

"We'll see them soon." Once again, the man's knuckles were white where he gripped the hammer. "Not much of an ambush, is it?"

"No, but that's no reason for us to simply stand here in the open."

"What do you mean?"

"Into the centre guard house – one side each," Never said. "I'm hoping they cannot sense either of us."

"They can't – I'm blocking them," he said. "The leader quests forth with his senses, generally I feel, rather than specifically seeking us."

"How long have you been doing that?" Never asked as they started toward the centre.

"Since I felt them – don't worry, it is no trouble."

"Good." Never paused. "I know you voiced some concern about your experience when it came to battle. You haven't faced many?"

"No."

"Then nothing I can say will prepare you. And we can plan all we like, but battle is all about reacting to what is going on around you. Things change fast and clinging to a plan that is no longer working is a swift path to death. Take your chances," he said. "And don't forget that I'm more than a match for those things."

The priest exhaled. "Even two of them?"

"Yes." Somehow, yes.

"That helps to hear you say, even though I know I am under the protection of God."

Never slapped him on the shoulder.

At the centre guard house, a soldier met them, crossbow in hand. "Father?"

"Dark forces are bound for this bridge," Father Lakiva said. "Flee."

The fellow blinked.

Never drew his knives and cut into his hands, letting the blood pool. "He's not exaggerating, soldier. Go, warn the city."

"But..."

"Go!" the priest shouted.

"Yes, Father." The man charged across the stones.

Lakiva straightened. "We need to take up positions. They're closing in."

"The guards at the other end," Never said, starting forward.

"There's no time."

"There is if I fly."

A rumbling stopped him before he took another step. Shouts rose from the far end of the bridge as a cloud of dust bore down on the span.

The faint snapping of crossbow bolts was quickly lost to the thundering of feet... and wheels – wheels from wagons drawn by hulking men with blue, stretched skin and jagged bone protrusions. Human cultists in red cloaks whipped the stakolin onward; the lead wagon bearing perhaps half a dozen men, all armed with spears. The second wagon carried only one man – he too with a blue taint to his skin but he was not as malformed as the 'animals' and wore a dark beard and a fine coat.

Why only one passenger? Unless...

"How do we stop them?" Father Lakiva cried.

"Leave the first one," Never replied as the creatures closed. "Sacha is in the second."

Father Lavika moved to the opposite guardhouse. "Are you sure?"

"Yes. Distract the stakolin," Never said as he let his wings burst free. Black feathers fluttered to the stone. He leapt onto the rail as the first wagon flashed by then swooped under the bridge. Shouts echoed but he ignored them; his focus had to stay on his gambit, which would take some serious timing. And luck.

He skimmed over the dark water then glided up in a rush of air, twisting as he rose above the span.

Below, the first wagon had already reached the far end of the bridge, but the second was slowing as it tried to avoid Father Lakiva, who was moving to block it at each adjustment. The priest had braced himself, his weapon encased in a pale nimbus – the Holy Thunder no doubt.

And lying across the back of the second wagon was a figure in silver armour, no helm covering her blond hair. Sacha.

Never plummeted down with a roar.

The driver twisted from his seat, jerking on the reins, but Never was too close – he swung his birch hand. His fist stuck with a mighty crack, throwing the man clear over the rail. Never caught a fleeting glimpse of the man's face as he flew through the air – the expression was one of rage rather than fear or shock.

But there was no time to dwell on it.

Never wheeled sharply, landing in the wagon bed with a thud – gripping the sides to slow his momentum, but his chest still slammed into the wood, causing the fire-stones Ayuni's mother had given him to dig into his flesh.

He gasped for air as the wagon rocked back, shuddering to a halt.

White light burst.

Father Lakiva had struck the stakolin with his hammer; the creature was still tangled in the wagon. Never bent to Sacha – her face was pale and blood matted the back of her hair when he lifted her, grunting at the weight.

She was not dead; of that he was sure.

He jumped down from the wagon and circled, giving the priest room.

The man swung a rapid succession of overhand blows upon the creature. The stakolin howled, a part-human, part-beast sound that chilled with its unnaturalness. It flinched back, swinging an elbow that crashed through the wagon.

Partially free now, it caught the next hammer blow.

The priest held steady, the light intensifying – but the creature did not yield, though it hissed and spat.

Never lowered Sacha to the bridge then sliced into his palm – only to stop at a shout.

"Cevana, seek Dromanev."

A line of cultists stood some distance away, one a little closer – hands folded within long red sleeves. Unlike the others, his hood was pushed back. He was a sallow-faced man yet his blue eyes were oddly placid.

The creature backed down at the cultist's words, giving

the wagon a shove with one hand. Wood screeched across tone. Then, the creature leapt away, breaking into a sprint, travelling back the way it came, heading for the river bank. To search for the cult leader? The bearded man, Dromanev?

Father Lakiva turned to face the Red Seed Cultist and Never stepped forward, blocking access to Sacha.

But the stranger only smiled, calling over his shoulder. "Bring the child."

A pair of the Svikamet half-dragged, half-carried a short figure forward. Temilo. The boy thrashed against them, expression fierce behind a gag. A small trail of blood rain from his scalp.

Never jabbed a finger at the leader. "Free him."

"No, Amouni. This is where your luck dries up. He is a fair exchange I think – and if you want to see him again, you will come to our home in the mountains."

"Or I take him back now." Never let a globe of crimson-fire snap up around his fist.

Now the man grinned, an almost lazy upturning of the lips. "You could do that or you could save Lady Isajan there."

"What?"

"She has ingested the *disrytha*. If you waste too much time fighting us now, she will either die or become stakolin. Of course, you could spend that time working on an antidote instead."

Never glanced at Father Lakiva. The priest stood ready, his own gaze hard. If it came to an attack, they could deal with the cultists easily enough... a blue-skinned figure rose from behind the others, eyes blazing yellow.

"We will await you most keenly," the leader said as he

turned.

"Wait," Never called.

"Yes?"

"Tell me now, that Temilo will not be harmed. Say the words."

"An oath?"

"Whatever you want to call it."

He chuckled. "Very well, let me assure you that the boy will not be harmed, so long as you come to Mount Siyapol."

Temilo gave the barest of nods.

"So be it. I will come."

"We are thrilled to hear you say so." The man waved to his supporters and they started back toward the road and their wagon, the beast turning back to glare at them.

Chapter 13.

Never leant over Sacha where she lay sweating atop her soft blue blankets, cup of water in hand. He'd hidden her in one of the better inns of Yusrina, the well-appointed room cold from the open window and, as befitting not only his forged document but Lakiva's status as priest, no-one had bothered them. Such grace would probably last until reports of what had happened on the bridge spread, but for now it seemed they had a little more time at least.

"I still think we will have better luck in the church," Lakiva said from where he paced the spacious room.

"So you have said," Never replied. "And you know what I believe."

"No-one will slay her as a precaution; that is not God's way."

"But can you speak for the High Priest here in Yusrina? Everyone else in the church? Can you be sure their fear – and it may be justified at that – will not lead them to do so?"

Before the man could answer, Sacha groaned.

Her eyes were fluttering.

"Sacha?"

Another groan and she opened her eyes fully. Upon seeing him, a deep frown followed. "Never?"

"Yes." He leant closer.

She lifted a hand slowly – then caught him by the throat. "The moment I am recovered I will kill you." She gasped the words out.

"Then you'd better get some rest first." Never removed her hand – breaking her grip was no struggle and he sat back with a sigh as Sacha closed her eyes once more. Not an unexpected reception, truly, but a little more vicious than he'd hoped.

"Perhaps it is you who needs protecting," Lakiva said.

"She'll see that it's a bad idea."

"Soon, I hope."

Never replaced the cup on the table he'd dragged to the bed. "Well, she won't get a chance to be angry with me again unless we can cure her."

The priest nodded. "Hence my belief the church is the right choice."

Never shook his head, though he could not say why, truly, he worried. The cult was obviously planning to transform Sacha; they'd given her the seeds well before the ambush on the bridge and so it was no feint to cover their retreat. And it also meant they didn't believe Temilo would be a likely candidate for becoming one of the stakolin – hence their willingness to tell the truth earlier.

All signs pointed to needing help.

But the Priesthood would hold her for observation, for research into the Svikamet and the process behind the red seeds. Even if it failed, they would want her. It would be irresponsible of them *not* to keep her.

And so handing her over would defeat the purpose of rescuing her in the first place.

Not that she'd bothered to show any gratitude.

"I saw something... while we travelled." Sacha spoke again.

Never turned. "About the seeds?"

"Yes." She swallowed. "I need water."

He held the mug to her lips. She swallowed, even as her hand replaced Never's. When she finished, she handed it back. "I can hold a cup, fool."

"Good to know."

She glared at him yet didn't seem able to rise – perhaps a good thing.

"What did they say, Lady Isajan?" Lakiva asked.

Sacha looked to the priest, taking in his white robes and the glimpse of chain mail beneath. "Little, Father. But Dromanev drinks from a vial at regular intervals." She paused to catch her breath. "It was a dull yellow colour. I think I could smell the scent of... vanilla."

"You think he uses it to maintain his humanity?"

She nodded. "That ingredient cannot be all of it, surely... but he is far more human than the others, so it must have some counter-effect on the seed."

"Could it be a place to start nevertheless?" Lakiva asked.

Never stood. "I certainly hope so – though I don't imagine just any merchant will sell vanilla here. It's not exactly the right climate."

"If any would have such a precious luxury, it would be the Duke."

"Then I'm off to the palace – watch her, Lakiva."

"Wait," Sacha said.

He paused.

"You must promise me something." Much of the fog had lifted from her eyes, the determination burned now.

"What?"

"If you cannot prevent me from becoming... like them, you will kill me first."

Never frowned. "A noble but needlessly dramatic sentiment, My Lady."

"Promise me!" she shouted, lifting herself onto a half-sitting position. Yet she could not hold it, and fell back into the pillows, breathing hard.

"I promise."

Never strode to the door, pulling it open and starting along the hall, his footfalls muffled by a heavy rug.

A voice followed him – Lakiva. "Never, do you know what you're doing?"

"Heading to the palace. And don't worry, no-one will see me unless I want them to," he said before pausing. "Father?"

"Yes?"

"This will sound like a threat – but if I return and Sacha has been moved to one of your churches, I will not be pleased."

"Fear not, I will follow your wishes."

"Good." Never turned into the short hall before the stairs, passing a serving girl with a tray of steaming broth, and made his descent. In the common room, its tables decorated with painted knucklebones and fangs for the gambling tournament ahead, he was met by a valet. "Can we help you, sir? A recommendation for entertainment in the city perhaps? There are many fine establishments that will even accept a foreigner with your connections."

"Actually, does the cook have any vanilla beans?"

"Sadly not – our supply has been cut off by the war."

"I understand."

"Is there anything else?"

"No. Simply continue to ensure no-one disturbs my room."

He inclined his head. "Of course."

Never ignored the glances he drew from the patrons and their silver forks as he headed into the night air. He quickened his pace, leaving the well-lit streets and the fur-lined faces of the people who sung joyful words meant to ward off the winter, and found a dark alley with a heap of crates stacked at the far end.

There, a figure grumbled from beneath the refuse when Never climbed the wood, but he launched himself into the night without bothering to check on the unfortunate fellow.

Below, people still filled the streets, firelight and singing chasing him. Across the dark rooves, the palace loomed like a great tower, spots of light from its windows spiralling up and around. Quite a pleasing image, really.

Never flew toward it, aiming for one of the darkened balconies.

He landed on the stone and paused to listen – no sounds from beyond the balcony windows. He drew a blade, pricked his finger and let a tongue of crimson-fire free. Then, he slid his fingertip along the glass, melting it enough to let his hand pass through and quickly unhook the latch. Never stepped into the dark room, boots muffled by the heavy carpeting.

The red glow revealed closet, basin and bed – and a figure rising from the sheets, eyes glittering in fear. It was a girl and her whole body was trembling.

"I'm not here to hurt anyone," Never said softly.

She shrank back.

Would she cry out? He strode for the door, glancing over his shoulder. "If you can avoid mentioning this to anyone for a while, that'd be most welcome."

Still, the girl did not react.

He opened the door and listened, peering into the shadowy hall – the nearest lamp seemed some distance away. He slipped outside and strode toward an intersection, passing suits of armour and plaques listing the names of soldiers who'd died in this war or that. Typical Vadiya decorations, a little unimaginative but speaking of strength and honour for those who had fallen.

The next hallway had been lit by twin lamps – far less satisfactory for sneaking about. A pair of servants giggled as they hurried around the far corner, and then he was alone. He followed their voices until they stopped – and in the next stone passage found no hint of the two, nor the sound of their voices.

Instead, a deep rumble began.

He moved forward, coming to a halt at a curious doorway, and from which the sound rose. Rather than an actual door, he faced a rectangular opening to a dark plunge with a mighty chain. The only thing stopping anyone from falling within was a small wooden gate. He leant a little closer, and evenly spaced shafts of light descended, hitting the black of the chain.

For climbing the palace? It had to be, considering how quickly the girls had disappeared. Impressive if that was its purpose – so too the counterweights that must have existed somewhere within the palace. Perhaps not surprising that the invention had not escaped Vadiya.

Booted footsteps approached – moving at speed.

Never took half a step for the opposite corner before stopping. Too far; they'd see him. "Something else." He wheeled on the shaft. "Perfect."

Never leapt within and caught the chain.

It swung a little, but he was able to climb up and out of the light, where he paused.

The thump of booted feet drew near and just as quickly they passed, shadows flashing. Never sighed – the girl had obviously told *someone* that he'd broken into her room. And no doubt the melted glass had caused something of an upset. Hard not to blame them.

Still, time to move a little quicker.

He slid down the chain enough to swing into the corridor, and then he was running on his toes, scanning the walls for a stairwell – *there*. Never slipped within and half-ran, half-leapt down the dim stair, one hand on the wall for balance.

At a door to the lower floor, he paused to listen. Nothing.

An empty passage lay beyond, similar to the others, and stepped directly into the next stairwell. "You should have chosen a window on the lower floors," he muttered.

And down he continued until pausing at a door to another lower floor, he grinned. The scent of bread was strong in the dim corridor... a kitchen. Never quickened his pace once more, following his nose now, only slowing for each corner until he came across a bright entryway.

Wide double doors stood ajar; the scent of baking bread strong now.

Word of his illicit entry into the palace wouldn't have reached the kitchen and so a different approach might be best, more bluffing perhaps.

Never passed through the doors and affected an expression of great agitation as he strode into a warm kitchen, comforting glow from stoves and cauldrons filling the room. It splashed itself across the white aprons and glinted on knives and other utensils. Cracking and thumping filled the room too, as the cooks and servants worked to prepare the morning meals – but none of it quick enough to drown out the sweet humming from a nearby woman.

"Kayla, are you nearly done?" someone called.

"Yes, chef," the humming woman said.

"Excuse me, madam?" Never asked. He ran a hand through his hair, pitching his voice a little too high.

She turned, eyes widening a little when she saw that he was not Vadiyem, but his command of the language was obviously enough to convince her that he probably belonged, because she greeted him with a hesitant smile. "Yes?"

He sighed in relief. "I've been sent all the way to the palace by My Lord; he's demanding something with vanilla."

"Oh." She frowned.

"It's a little unusual, I know," he said, shaking his head as if in disbelief. "But as *jenaek* I suppose he feels *I* should run such errands at all hours of the night. No matter that I've served Lord Jasul faithfully for near ten years now."

"Ah... I don't know that we have anything prepared."

Never groaned.

"But perhaps we could make something – if he could wait?"

"I don't know."

"Hmmm. What if you took some vanilla beans back? I'm sure your Lord's cook would be able to whip something up."

"*That* is a brilliant idea," Never told her.

"I'll be back in just a moment," Kayla said, beaming as she left.

Never leant against the wall with a sigh – and this time it was no act; he had the vanilla now, the question was, would it make any difference when he took it back to Sacha?

Chapter 14.

Never watched as Sacha placed the cup down, blinking against the dawn light where it poured through the window. A plate of cold broth sat beside her, but she only glanced at it as she sat straighter in the bed. "I *do* feel a little better. Not well enough to keep that down... but better."

"Well enough to ride?" Never asked. "Or should we get a cart?"

"I will be able to ride."

"I am glad it's working," he said.

"You shouldn't be."

He frowned at her tone. "Thinking of your ill-advised promise, are you?"

She narrowed her eyes as she swung her legs over the bed, but did not stand – doubtless she could not yet do so. "I am always thinking of it."

"Well put it aside until you're strong enough to do something about it," Never said. "And while you're doing that – put it aside again until we can stop the Svikamet and save Temilo."

She glared at him. "No."

"Fine." He folded his arms. "Feel free to follow me and Lakiva south when you can. Once I save your entire nation, you can face me and I will cast you down too, if that is truly what you seek."

"Arrogant fool."

"So, do you still want that ride?"

"Yes," she hissed.

"Then call for the priest if you need anything – I'm going to arrange for a steed befitting the Lady Isajan," Never said as he left the room.

He swept through the corridors, down the stairs and into the city. Father Lakiva had called from the common room, but Never did not answer. Instead, he strode through the empty streets, the chill morning air crisp enough to cut his skin as he walked.

But he soon found a horse merchant and a mare that didn't seem aggressive, nor so placid that it would fail to able to keep up. And despite his haggling, it took the last of his shards to purchase the horse. It hardly mattered, truly – with Sacha, or with Lakiva, he'd not have to pay for much more in Vadiya.

Before he could return to the inn, a pair of figures strode into the street before him. Both held crossbows; one was unshaven and the other a little more groomed, despite the faded clothing. But their weapons were well-cared for and held with assurance, though even from a distance the scent of whiskey hung on the air.

"That's a fine animal there, *jenaek*," one said, speaking in Marlosi.

"Isn't it?" Never replied in Vadiyem as he stepped in

front of the mare. "I was impressed by the glossy coat – I imagine such discerning gentlemen as yourselves are too."

The clean-shaven man sneered. "Clever bastard, aren't you?"

"Yes. But a better question is – are you?"

"Here's your final chance, fool," the unshaven fellow said, raising the weapon.

Never clenched his jaw. Thrashing a pair of thugs would have been most welcome after facing Sacha's utter lack of gratitude, her stubbornness, but crossbow bolts were not so easy to catch. Still...

"I have a counter offer you might be interested in," Never said.

"Let's hear it," Shaven snickered.

"Right, and we'll take whatever you have in mind too," Unshaven added.

"If I can bend the blade of my belt knife with my bare hand, you let me go free. If not, I give you the horse and the last of my silver."

Shaven laughed. "That so? What do you think, Fedif?"

"I think I'd like to see him cut himself up before we rob him, sure."

"You are both so generous," Never said. "I'll just reach for a knife now."

"Please do."

Never drew a blade and gripped it in one hand, holding it out before him and letting the edge slice into his forefinger. Blood trailed into his palm and he grinned. "Ready?"

"Of course we are," Fedif said with a smirk.

Crimson-fire burst around his fist. It shot forth in a stream of blazing light, hissing in the cold air. The fire tore through the space between the men, who leapt back with shouts. Shaven was babbling but Fedif could not speak at all, gaping from where he'd landed on the stones of the street.

"Now run," Never snapped.

They scrambled to their feet with cries, and charged down the stones – Fedif a little less steady. Never let the crimson-fire die away before resuming his walk, leading the somewhat skittish horse behind him.

Yet when he neared their inn he slowed – a ring of soldiers surrounded the *Duke's Bounty*, these men seeming a mix of infantry, mercenary and even two Steelhawks, their arsenal of weapons clearly setting them apart. All in all, it seemed to be near two-score men.

The leader beat a fist upon the doors to the inn, raising his voice. "We know you harbour cultists – bring them to us or we will break this door down."

Moving slowly but not stopping, Never turned into the mouth of an alley, stroking the horse's neck as he did.

The innkeeper seemed to be refusing, though there was some confusion in his tone.

"You may believe that to be true – and God willing it actually is – but we must be sure and you will not prevent us performing our duty," came the reply from the leader of the soldiers.

Never tied the horse's lead rope to a drainpipe and ran to the end of the alley where he once again let his wings free and climbed up and out of the streets, landing on the roof before glancing back toward the Bounty. If he circled wide enough, keeping fairly low, he'd be able to reach the rear of the inn.

There was a chance he'd be seen by early risers but getting Sacha and Lakiva out was more important. He leapt from the roof, swooping into the streets but keeping near the rooves, beating hard to keep aloft, passing sleeping wagons and crates before landing on the stable's roof.

Horses nickered. He ran forward and leapt from the edge of the stable. He flew to the windows, beating his wings long enough to find the right one, before swinging into the room.

Lakiva spun, the white nimbus snapping up around him, and Sacha did the same from where she'd pressed her ear against the door.

"Never, what's happening?" she demanded. "I can hear shouting."

"Steelhawks and other soldiers. They want to be sure you aren't a stakolin."

She swore.

"I could convince them," Lakiva offered.

"Let's not risk it," Never said. "I'll fly us out of here. I have a horse nearby; we can leave the city before everyone wakes."

"Fly us?" Lakiva asked.

"Yes. Right now."

"Take Sacha, I can climb down. I should be able to manage the stable yard wall too."

"Right." Never held out his hand to Sacha. "Ready?"

"How?" Sacha said as she left the door. Shouts and the crashing of boots filled the downstairs.

Never leapt out the window and beat his wings, gaining enough height. "I'll catch you."

She frowned but climbed onto the sill and launched herself up with a wince she tried to hide.

Their wrists smacked together. He beat his wings again, harder, to keep them dipping too far, and slowly turned toward the stable. Once he'd gained enough height, Never glided down over the rooves and twisted around to a backstreet close to the horse.

There, he slowed their descent, doing his best to let Sacha reach the ground softly, then he hit the stone beside her. "Hopefully Lakiva marked our path."

Sacha nodded but again did not speak.

Never swallowed a retort.

Chapter 15.

"I'm sorry, I wanted to bring our horses but the Steelhawks were too close," Lakiva said between breaths when he stood before them. Light was growing in the alley where Never had hid the horse – but thus far, they hadn't been found. Time, however, was not on their side.

"We'll manage," Never replied. "Better to be free on foot."

"And now?" Sacha asked.

Never untied the mare and gestured to the saddle. "Do you need—"

"No." She lifted a foot into the stirrup, gripped the pommel and swung herself into the saddle with a grunt. But she took the reins without complaint, appearing steady enough.

"Let's circle to the south from the western gate," Lakiva said. "That way we won't have to cross into territory they might be searching."

"If we can keep ahead of them, that should work," Sacha said.

"And then?"

"We set up camp in the plains – there are ruins south of the city, or if we are lucky, we'll reach a village before nightfall."

Never crept to the mouth of the alley and peered out – enough of the vigilante force remained before the *Duke's Bounty* that there was a good chance leaving the alley unseen would be impossible. "I'm going to distract them; make for the gate," he said.

"How?" Sacha was frowning. "If you make too big of a disturbance, you'll have them on our tail the whole way south."

"No-one will see my wings," he said, then ran back for the rear of the alley where he took to the skies again – only to land on the roof. Then he ran across the black tiles, boots scraping, but he kept his balance as he approached the inn, still a few buildings away.

The space between homes was not so great that he couldn't leap across; he did so until he found himself on the Bounty's roof, where he paused to catch his breath. Muffled shouts were clear from the rooms below but also the stable; where people were searching the stalls – the soldiers had obviously found their mounts.

Yet they'd learn little they didn't already know.

Never dropped to a crouch and crept to the opposite end of the building that overlooked the street. To his left, a little farther away, what seemed to be a fletcher's shop, living quarters in the second storey above, and to the right, the alley where Sacha and Lakiva waited.

"Time to test my legs."

Never felt around for a loose tile, wrenching it free before tossing it down to the cobblestones and rising. "I take it you're all looking for me?" he called.

Half a dozen men spilled into view, faces shocked where they clutched their weapons. "It's the *jenaek*," one shouted.

Never grinned as he spun and sprinted for the edge of the roof.

He leapt for the fletcher. Air rushed around him and he landed with a grunt, breaking into a roll, another tile spilling free. Then he was on his feet once more, using the momentum to charge and jump to the next roof – this one much closer.

Shouts followed him from the ground. He turned, now aiming for what seemed to be another home, the building would give him access to a nearby warehouse – and more importantly, the giant walled enclosure. Within waited rows of silent wagons and carts.

The only problem being that the wall was some distance away and he couldn't use his wings. Below, the thunder of boots kept pace – he'd be seen, and every moment let the sun rise higher, let the chance of being spotted by more people increase too.

Yet little could be done about it... he had to leave them behind.

Killing them all wouldn't have been impossible – not with the crimson-fire... but were their lives so cheap? All the fools wanted was to protect their city from a dire threat. Going down there and incapacitating them all was too risky too, quick healing or no.

It left his wings.

"Damn." Never let his feathers free, then bent to a crouch before thrusting up, beating his wings hard enough to stir dust. He shot into the air, climbing directly up and up until the city walls began to shrink. Perhaps the search party was still down there pointing to the sky and crying out, but if nothing else, he could ascend beyond their eyesight and then they'd not be able to trace his flight – he'd bank around and approach the city from the west.

Hopefully Sacha and Lakiva had made their escape.

***

Never strode up the paved road beneath the warm sun, skipping around a wagon train laden with fruit and vegetables, to approach a white-robed man leading a horse, the rider shielding her eyes against the sun.

He stopped, stepping off the road and into the dirt to wait for them to draw level.

"No problems?" he asked.

"Obviously not," Sacha replied.

Never shook his head. "We need to find the river – I want to get to Vitrii as soon as possible."

"Another ambush?" Lakiva asked.

"Not this time – I think we need to be a little more prepared and the stakolin are obviously far, far swifter than I estimated."

"They can cover a lot of ground at a sustained pace – we once tracked one who covered in days what took us an entire week," Sacha said. "And if you mean the Argov then think again. I'm not going to row that far upstream, Never."

"Nor will you," he said, not bothering to explain. The Argov was perfect, it ran from the mountains, passed Vitrii and eventually fed into Yusrina Lake – which meant a direct path to their destination. Now, all that remained was to find a smaller river or creek that branched from it.

"You mean something to do with your heritage."

"Yes. Let's keep moving; maybe there's some water near those ruins you mentioned."

Never set off at a jog without waiting to see if they were following; keeping a similar pace and offering few breaks as they passed more fields of wheat and farmhouses set off the road.

Clouds swept in before noon, bringing a cold wind with them, though no rain fell as they left the road to eat the few trail-rations Lakiva had collected before leaving Yusrina. Never sat apart, the chill from the fallen log he was using quickly seeping through his cloak and pants.

Sacha was going to be a problem.

Even now, as she and Lakiva sat together where they boiled the vanilla beans over a small fire, she stared across at him. Difficult not to stare back – what did she want, truly? Revenge? Obviously, more than her pride had been hurt that day.

And yet... Snow had made his own choices.

Never turned away with a small sigh. It was all somewhat childish... but Sacha *had* lost someone she loved. "As did I." And despite the imbecility of any potential fighting between them, especially while they needed to work together, it wasn't out of character for Sacha. Her will was iron.

After she'd taken another dose, they broke their tiny camp and travelled until dusk. The thin ruins of an old outpost came into view – part stone tower, part grassy knoll. Yet no smoke rose from the crumbling roof; it seemed unoccupied.

"I'll find firewood," Never said, striding into the rest of

the ruin the moment they arrived.

"I'll set up inside," Lakiva replied, glancing between Never and Sacha but saying nothing.

Never's legs swished through the long grasses as he searched, pausing to scoop up the occasional stray branch – it was slim pickings, since generations of travellers had done a comprehensive job already. In places, oak trees grew between broken paving stones, some half-sheltered by the old walls, and they offered some fuel at least.

Nothing useable remained in the outpost; it was grass, moss, and half-buried stone and in one building, a rusted trap door. He kicked at the handle.

"We need to talk before we reach Vitrii."

Sacha stood behind him, arms folded.

"Oh? Changed your mind about killing me then?"

"We have to find a way to cooperate if you truly want to help my people."

He set the wood down and leant against one of the low stone walls. He ignored the way she had established *herself* as the one forced to reason with a stubborn fool. "I will do what I must to stop the stakolin."

"I do not doubt you, Never – you always had a strong sense of duty."

"As do you," he said. "But even as you say that, I can tell you *do* doubt me."

"You aren't sharing everything."

"Meaning?"

"The mode of travel you promise for one. Also, whatever you suspect about the creatures. It does not encourage trust."

"Are you saying you believe you *can* trust me? That you

can set everything aside?"

"I can try." Her expression did not waver.

If they were to work well together, it was a step, perhaps not a large one, but she'd been the one to take it. And locking her out of his thinking, and Lakiva by extension, was a mistake. He nodded. "Let's talk over a meal."

Chapter 16.

"This outpost once served to warn Yusrina of attacks from the south-west," Lakiva said, pointing to the half-broken symbol on the wall, that of an elk. His voice seemed loud in the hush of the tower, the stones appearing warmer beneath the flow of firelight. "A long time ago now, when the two fiefdoms fought over the lake and the hardwood in the forests."

"Is that where you recommend we travel next?" Never asked. "To the forests?"

"No, we could reach a river sooner, I think, if we turn east. It's been a while since I saw a map, to tell the truth."

"That is correct," Sacha said. She sat before the fire, hands outstretched. Sweat beaded at her temples but it was not the fire so much as the fever she still fought; her dose of vanilla due soon. Whether it was working enough was debatable – on one hand, she had not turned into a stakolin nor had she died.

Yet she was not at her full strength, either.

Dromanev's concoction obviously bore more than the

vanilla bean.

Never had already explained the use of the river and the Amouni guides, along with all that he knew or suspected about the cult – as had Lakiva – but together, they had not yet come up with a solid plan. The stakolin were near impervious to steel and fire and it took many men – or a single Amouni with some help – to stop just one.

What would happen if three or four or a dozen attacked?

"We need to understand the seeds themselves," Never said. "What did you discover?" he asked Sacha.

"All of the plants we suspect they used were stripped of any fruit or seed, then poisoned somehow."

"Those from the lake?"

"Yes. We also found two near a mountain pool – also useless."

"I had been wondering if I shouldn't quickly fly across to the lake but now I wonder if it would be worthwhile."

"Perhaps not," she replied. "Father may have made some strides – his priests are hard at work, aided by the High Priest himself."

"Truly?" Lakiva asked.

"Yes. Before I left on my failed quest of extermination, they were confident of understanding more."

Never nodded. "Then our path remains – we seek water and then Vitrii, to consult the High Priest, though I fear I might predict something they discover."

"What is that, Never?" Sacha asked.

"That this all has something to do with Amouni bloodlines."

Lakiva frowned. "But how? Are you not the last?"

Never did not look at Sacha, though he caught a glimpse

of her from the edge of his vision; she turned away. "Of a special bloodline, yes. But there is much left in the world that I have not encountered. What if someone – perhaps Dromanev – stumbled across something in the depths of Siyapol?" And what if Snow had somehow been responsible? After all, it wasn't as though the man had been adverse to experimenting. Yet Never did not share that thought, nor would he have, with or without Sacha present.

"Do you believe he survived?" Lakiva asked.

Never nodded. "That cultist wouldn't have sent the other creature after him if there wasn't a chance."

"Given their strength and stamina, I would agree," Sacha said. "Despite how cruel the falls of Kraidav." She drew and lifted her sword. "Yet we shouldn't forget this. They want *you*, Never."

"Right. And doesn't that hint at some connection between what they are and my ancestors?"

Father Lakiva nodded. "That's not an unreasonable connection to draw."

"Then it's my responsibility to put a stop to it," Never said.

"Let's reach home first," Sacha said, drawing a deep breath after speaking.

"You need to rest, My Lady," Lakiva said.

"Perhaps."

"I will take first watch." Never rose. He paused, meaning to ask if Sacha was all right... but instead, he left the tower. She'd only resent the question; typical Vadiya pride.

The night was cold enough that he soon found himself stamping his feet, trying to warm his toes. And it would only get worse, the further south they travelled. "Autumn, you had better cling to the land a little longer." Clouds still covered the sky, letting no moon or starlight free and so he leant against the stone and listened.

Faintly, the chirping of some bug but nothing else from outside – and only small sounds within the tower.

Never circled the camp twice during his watch – once from the sky – but saw and sensed nothing. The supposed emptiness of the area brought some comfort; the creature from the marsh which had simply waited and watched not far from his mind.

Had it been one of the stakolin? Dromanev himself?

If the other creatures had trouble controlling themselves, that man did not seem to be of the same ilk. If it had been truly stakolin in the marsh. There was a slim chance it could have been a wild animal... though it seemed unlikely.

An equally troubling question was exactly *how* or at what point the cult knew he was in Vadiya?

How long had they been planning whatever it was they wanted him for?

Had Lord Taginus been no more than the first piece of bait?

And thus Sacha the second... and even if they had also planned to turn her, was that her role? Bait? Just as Temilo was now? Either way, he had another responsibility. "Hold on, little guy," Never said. "We're coming for you."

Chapter 17.

Another dark river cutting through the plain, another cruel wind, another cloud-plagued sky above, another horse set free, and now another Guide standing perfectly still before him. Unlike many of the Guides found in other parts of the world, this robed woman and her fish head were drawn in sharp relief where she stood in the water, feet disappearing where the flow ran across smooth rocks.

Her voice, too, was strong – and yet the same startling difference was present here: half her robe was blue, half white. As though two Guides had been joined.

Her flat voice echoed within his mind.

Of course, I can take you all there. Please, clasp my hand, Master.

Never gripped Sacha's hand, who in turn held Lakiva, then he reached for the Guide.

A sinking feeling followed, black swallowing him, despite the relative shallowness of the small river. Yet it made no difference to the Guide, nor the lights that rose, flashing in long streaks of green and blue.

As ever, the passage of time was unclear, but once they stood upon the banks of the Argov, a light covering of snow spread across the road and the woods too. The tall pines were near-black, but not because of the light; that was simply their hue. They screened any view of Sacha's city, but it was only a short walk.

This time, thankfully, no travellers were nearby to witness their appearance. Nor be soothed by Lakiva's holy voice.

Never thanked the Guide and it faded away.

"That was... disconcerting," Sacha said.

"But effective," Never replied. "Straight to the Keep then?"

She nodded. "Father will have something to share."

Sacha led them along the paved road and into the trees, which reared up to cast needles down in silence; they littered the ground here, sharp against the patches of snow. Never smothered a sigh as he walked, breath steaming in the air.

The trees soon parted to reveal the city of Vidrii, which seemed to be a part of the very mountains themselves; a huge drawbridge had been lowered over a crevice that ringed the city.

Catapults loomed on the walls and towers climbed up beyond; thin white stone topped with black, peaked rooves and upon them, ringed balconies that sported massive, mounted crossbows capable of flinging trunk-sized bolts.

Compared to the delicate-seeming bridges between the towers, all the weaponry might have looked out of place – yet it had always been such a city, supposedly Vitrii had been built by ancient stone wrights with skills long since lost, and only become more war-like as Vadiya itself changed.

The pale keep was no exception – it, too, was well-fortified where it rested above the city, and behind its walls was a half-circle of progressively smaller towers that spread out from a central dome, black tiles unbroken by any openings. A long time since he'd set foot within; how different things had been between them back then.

They'd loved each other in that mix of abandon and reserve, unable to speak plainly and more, hiding things from each other... had she always enjoyed more, the thrill of defying her father? Yet, it was no better hiding the hope that she would be the key to escape.

"The Pride of the South," Sacha said, pausing to stare up at her home. Her expression was somewhat fierce and the fever seemed to have receded completely.

"I can see why," Lakiva replied.

At the draw bridge a pair of Steelhawk guards met them – both First Rangers by the numeral insignia their armour, which rested by the red talon of House Isajan. Both snapped to attention upon seeing their mistress.

One grinned in what seemed to be relief. "My Lady!"

"The whole city has been worried," the other said. "I can send a runner?"

"Yes. And a carriage."

He blinked. "You are wounded?"

"In a manner of speaking."

"Of course, My Lady – forgive me for prying." He bowed then charged across the draw bridge, his heavy footfalls having no impact on the mighty structure.

"Space will be made in the guardhouse, My Lady," the remaining guard said.

"Perfect," she said, and once more, perhaps a little slower than before, led them forward. Never watched her a moment. Perhaps his earlier assessment of her improving health had been too hasty.

The guardhouse was empty – at least, it became so once it was known that Lady Isajan had returned; the armoured men and women all too happy to leave the warm hearth and stand in the cold.

Never moved close to the fire to wait for the carriage but it arrived quickly and he barely got a chance to truly warm up. But at least their path was taken in comfort, the lush cushions and sleek thoroughfares providing a smooth ride up and through the city.

So much was familiar; the way every other inn bore a hawk in its name or sign, the spruce and fir trees growing behind steel fences, some trunks straining the bounds, the way the women here wore their hair shorter than in the north, the dominance of reed pipes – even the old song about a man who saved his family from a fire only to drown in the river, something he'd heard performed as a comedy and as a tragedy... almost fond memories.

Even as a prisoner.

And it hadn't all been for naught; of course the rumour of an ancient Vadiya temple beneath the city had proven fruitless, but in exchange for failure, for being captured by the Isajans – he had met Sacha.

Though truthfully, had that ended up becoming its own misfortune?

Time would tell.

He frowned. And time would tell something else too – something he'd foolishly overlooked – Lord Dakan Isajan. Would the old fox have accepted Never's escape yet? It was more than a few years past now. Even if the man hated to be outsmarted, surely he had bigger concerns now?

Sacha was smiling at him. "You look like you've bitten into something sour."

"Perhaps I have."

"I think I can guess what it is – you're wondering how my father will respond to your return?"

"Indeed. Any ideas?"

She shrugged. "I couldn't say – we rarely spoke of you after your escape."

"Ah."

"You know, back on the Hanik border, I wanted to ask you something, Never."

"You did?"

"Yes. How *did* you escape? The keep here was and is very, very secure."

"How about I make you a deal?"

"Namely?"

"Prevent your father from trying to clap me in irons again and I'll tell you."

"Hmmm – he's quite wilful."

He nodded. "Yes, a polite word for *stubborn* – like daughter, like father. But in that case, my secret stays with me."

"I'm serious; I don't know how he'll respond, though he will accept your aid. He won't abandon his duty to the people."

"That's not of great comfort."

The carriage was drawing near to the palace now; clear due to the large square, its sides lined with merchants and the stalls for recruitment, Steelhawks standing before them, armour gleaming. But it was the dozens of figures in the black and red-striped livery that suggested the palace was near, as the servants faced the cold to gather what their masters would not.

"Trust me," she said.

"Hmmm."

Father Lakiva cleared his throat. "Forgive me, but will Lord Isajan truly seek to detain Never?"

"He may. Never was once our prisoner here, many years past."

"You were?"

Never nodded. "Her Ladyship here was the only thing that made it bearable, to be honest."

"Then you were once... ah, that is, you…"

"Yes, Father Lakiva," Sacha said. "We were but once again; that will not be a problem. Father may not have approved at all, but he will do what is right for our people."

And soon enough the truth of her words would become clear.

Chapter 18.

Lord Dakan Isajan met them not in the nobleman's fine rooms with their many fireplaces and red drapery, not even a draft-ridden but walled reception hall, but outside beneath the wan sun where he stood on the palace parapets, leather-bound arm outstretched as he waited for his hawk to return.

The reunion with his daughter had been surprisingly informal for the Lord – Never even thought he detected a tear as the man embraced her – and even more surprisingly, Dakan had not called for guards upon seeing Never.

Not that such a call would have been a problem precisely – escaping a cell would not have been a problem, but it would have made a bad impression to escape twice and truly, Never needed the Lord's cooperation.

"Never of Marlosi," Sacha's father eventually said. His beard was white now but he still stood tall despite the limp, a black cloak covering his breastplate, sword belted at his side. His blue eyes had not lost any of their vigour, either.

"Lord Dakan."

"You appear to be in fine health compared to when I last saw you – somewhat more at peace, even."

Never raised an eyebrow. Interesting – both the welcome and the words themselves. "It did not realise I gave such an impression."

"And I must thank you and Father Lakiva for saving my daughter."

"Of course, Lord Isajan," Lakiva said. "We appreciate your hospitality."

"Please take advantage of it, Father. I believe High Priest Firalod will join us for the evening meal; he is actually conducting services now if you wish to join him."

"Thank you," Lakiva said, and excused himself; heading for the distant stairwell, the cold breeze pulling at his white robe.

"Sacha, I know your mother would like to see you; she is still abed," Dakan said.

She straightened. "Is she unwell?"

"Nothing to fear; she is just fatigued of late."

"Good." Sacha made to follow the priest, but she paused to look up to her father. "You're being awfully calm – I trust that's not going to change once you send me away?"

"No, daughter," he said with a smile, and it seemed he was amused that *she* was taking a more parent-like tone. "You have made it clear how vital Never is to our cause."

As she left, Sacha gave Never a look that told him he had been wrong.

Something he was pleased about.

"I must thank you again, Never," Dakan said as he stared across the city. "I would not once have considered demanding that she refrain from personally defending her people – she is too proud and to be honest, she is too great a soldier and leader... but these stakolin concern even me. When we lost contact with her my hope grew weak."

"I understand your concern."

The older man turned to face him. "Then you will understand this – I expect you to protect her. I will not stop her heading into the mountains, but you can watch over her. If even half the stories about the war are true, you can do what I cannot. And if you fail, I will have your head, Amouni or not."

"I believe you mean that, My Lord," Never said. "I had wondered where the man I remembered had gone."

He snorted. "Mistake not my growing sentimentality for weakness – it only makes me fiercer."

In truth, Never owed Sacha nothing... yet he couldn't refuse the man and it would not be a lie. He didn't mean for Sacha, Lakiva, for anyone to die. Maybe it was an old burden but one it seemed he had long-since accepted. The risks were the same but he was no longer the same man, tortured and unsure. He was Ascended Amouni, the last.

The creatures did not know what they were asking for when they demanded he come to their lair.

"I will stop them and Sacha will return."

"That is of comfort, Never. Now, why don't you take some time to yourself before we eat – simply find a servant, they have been given instructions."

"Thank you, My Lord."

Never left the man to await his hawk and strode across the parapets, ducking into the doorway, the chill from the wind easing. His footsteps echoed in the stairwell as he wound his way down. Soon, another set of steps joined his – someone ascending, and at speed.

A blond figure appeared; her face familiar. Someone from his time in the keep before? Her expression was not welcoming. And while she was no soldier, like all in Vadiya, she was armed – but she carried something small and rectangular.

"You!" she cried between breaths.

Never frowned.

"You took him from me, you filthy *jenaek*!" she said as she neared.

"Who are you?" he asked.

But she did not answer, had she heard him at all? Instead, she thrust whatever she held into his face – it was a painting, the edges crumpled but it did not obscure the portrait, a cruel, haughty image.

And it too, quite familiar.

Commander Harstas.

"He was my brother and you murdered him. Do you even know what you did to me? To our family? We are ruined now," she cried, and a rage filled her voice where it bounced from the walls.

Yet Never only shook his head. "You expect what from me?"

"What I expect? Retribution – you are a monster!"

He folded his arms. An old insult, not one he'd heard in some time, but it hurt just the same. And he was done. "Here is what I offer," Never said. "Nothing. Absolutely nothing."

She blinked, choking on her next words.

"Please stand aside."

Still perhaps in shock, she did. He strode passed, yet he'd only taken half a dozen steps before her voice rang out again.

"Murderer!"

He spun, hands clenched tight. "I told you – you will receive nothing from me; *I cleaned the lands of the stain that he was.* A man that devoted his life to greed and death, a man who used his might to kill others instead of protecting them, a man that joined a needless war as a cover for his greed – do you even understand what that means? He left his home and family to enter another land to kill other families. That is the man you fight for now?"

"No, that isn't –"

"It is. And do you know that instead of facing the Bakar in the forest, he threw one of his men in their path – that is your brother, and he barely deserved the swift death I gave him!"

She gasped out a sob. "None of that mattered – they, they were only *jenaek*, they deserved to die."

Never leapt up the steps with a roar. "Why?"

But she had already collapsed into a heap, the painting clutched to her chest as she wailed.

Never unclenched his fists and turned away; she was nothing more than a fool.

He started back down the stairs, blood still thumping in his ears. His words rang loud and cruel: I cleaned the lands of the stain that he was. A little too close to something Snow would have said. And yet, Harstas was all of the things Never had claimed.

And the man's sister seemed near as bad. She, too, believed people of other lands were lesser.

Yet her grief... that at least he understood; it could make anyone a fool.

Never slowed before reaching the lower floor, taking

a moment to breathe. He needed to calm down – maybe whoever was to take him to his room would be delivering him to one that included a bath.

"That would do wonders."

But even if he had no luck there, anything was better than waiting around for the woman to return or for someone else to come searching for the source of all the shouting.

Chapter 19.

Lord Dakan and his regal wife, Lady Natasiv, sat at the head of the broad table that was laden with fish, fowl, beef and venison, vegetables and rich sauces too. There was no shortage of ale and wine, though Never only took water.

High Priest Firalod and Lakiva sat to the left of their hosts and Sacha closer to the right of her parents, Never finding himself beside her in turn.

While the Lady Natasiv was not so different to when he saw her last, still some years younger than her husband and blonde as her daughter, she now had shoulder-length hair and wore a look of concealed pain – though she was still gracious in welcoming him. "You have done God's work, Never – you are welcome here always."

It was High Priest Firalod that Never found himself considering more as they ate. The man was a thin, almost wraith-like with long features and a carefully-groomed beard of red. Outwardly, he appeared jovial but there was a sharpness to his gaze that bespoke his standing in the Vadiya Church.

In truth, the man was a welcome distraction from the encounter with Harstas' sister, who he had not yet seen again. The much-anticipated bath had done its work to clear the anger from his mind – for now, the vital concerns of the stakolin had to remain his focus.

Once the meal was cleared away and replaced by tea and fruit, High Priest Firalod explained the result of his research into the seeds. "We are certain it is a harmless species that has been cross-pollinated with something else, something unknown, and that its appearance on the Lake of Yusrina was no accident – Dromanev and his lackeys used the favourable summer to test their growth in the warmer climate. We estimate that as many as three-score plants were grown there."

"Bearing how much of the *disrytha*, High Priest?" Never asked.

"In our own now aborted attempts to grow a full specimen, we estimate any given plant might yield as many as one hundred good seeds."

Lord Dakan placed his cup down. "Which means at least a possible six thousand of those things ravaging the lands if we fail."

"What of the success rate?" Never asked. A dire threat... and something that couldn't be allowed to come to pass. No matter the cost. Such a force would likely overrun even the military might of Vadiya, given enough time. And then they would turn their attention to the rest of the world – if that was their purpose, and he had no reason to believe otherwise.

Dakan nodded. "Even providing for some of the ruined bodies we discovered, it is hard to judge whether they face three failures for every successful transformation. Perhaps it is one in ten. Whatever the rate of failure, we cannot count on it to be high enough to matter. Just a single stakolin is problem enough."

"Do you have any of them here?" Never asked. "Failures, I mean. I know you've already mentioned no living cultists as prisoner."

"One rests beneath the keep, yes," Dakan replied.

"I will show you, if you wish, Amouni," the High Priest offered.

"There's something we haven't discussed yet," Father Lakiva said, his face troubled. "I know in Karn we have not borne the brunt of the cult's madness. In fact, much of what we've done is rather academic in nature. I feel some guilt in knowing that, up until recently, it was a problem, a puzzle for me... but I have faced one now and everything has changed. I know we have spoken of conquest and the creation of an army, perhaps. But is that the whole purpose of the cult?"

"You refer to Sacha's abduction?" Dakan asked.

"I do. From a tactical standpoint, putting an end to the leader of any hunting party is sound, of course. But capturing her in order to transform her is a slightly more concerning goal – are they looking for stronger people?"

"Because the seeds do not work on just anyone?" Sacha said.

"We have wondered the same thing," her father replied.

Lakiva nodded. "And the logical extension of their goal would to be seek stronger and stronger subjects..."

"Like me," Never said.

Sacha's expression darkened. "That is not something we can allow."

"Then fear not – for I do not believe I can be turned," Never said. "And they have no way to know that, so perhaps we can use that to our advantage."

"You are sure, Never?" Dakan asked.

"Yes." In truth, he was not completely certain... but it did seem his body had well-and-truly rejected Taginus' poison. "My blood burned it away after we fought."

"That is a relief," the High Priest said, curiosity clear in his eyes.

"So how does that direct our next move?" Sacha asked. "What else did you learn?"

"We are no closer to finding their exact lair but we are watching. Considering their desire for Never, it is likely you will now no longer have to search too hard for it," Lord Dakan said.

Never hesitated with his next question. How much had Sacha told her father about her own fight against the *disrytha*? Presumably she was still taking the vanilla. "Did the study of the seed or beast themselves indicate any particular weaknesses? Anything that might counter the effects?"

"Little thus far, I am afraid," the High Priest said. "Of course, God's Thunder is effective but that is not something all can wield."

Lady Isajan leant forward. "There might be something. Our sons have been tracking a stakolin near the coast to the northwest. The last message contained something I found odd."

"The accident?" Dakan asked.

Sacha straightened in her chair. "Accident? What happened?"

"They were not hurt at that time, dear," Natasiv said. "But

Tavoya and his men chased one of the stakolin into a cave and believe that it disturbed a den of bats, and that their cries disoriented the creature, enabling them to cut it down with greater ease."

"Interesting but almost impossible to use in a battle, sadly," Sacha said.

"But we should keep it in mind," Never said. "Who knows what we will encounter in the mountains."

"Perhaps all that is left to decide is who to send with you," the High Priest said.

"As few as possible," Never replied. "Until we know exactly how many of them lurk within – or how to defeat them – we shouldn't risk too many lives."

"Hmmm." Lord Dakan stroked his beard.

"I'd say you were better off using your Hawks out here, protecting the cities and towns from the stakolin already roaming. Especially considering only priests and I can face them alone."

"You are not leaving me behind, Never," Sacha said.

"I know that."

"There is someone you may find useful already camped in the mountains," the High Priest said. "We left her there to assist the other priests in case of an attack but her special skills may prove useful if you are first seeking information only."

"Special skills?" Never asked.

"Indeed. Something my forebears have long forbidden but which the more pragmatic among us have nevertheless seen fit to make use of during the centuries; those which we do not share with the Light."

Lakiva gasped. "Holiness! Surely you do not mean..."

High Priest Firalod nodded. "The *nekromant*."

"Surely they are a myth?" Lady Isajan exclaimed.

"No, only hidden. The great shame of the Priesthood, I fear," the High Priest said, stroking his beard. "At present, only six are even active... but perhaps they will offer some insight, who knows? We have been hoping she could speak to a fallen creature."

"A death-walker?" Never asked.

"Yes, though it is better described as speaking with the dead rather than walking with them," the High Priest said.

"But they can actually raise the dead?"

"After fashion – it is easier to witness than have me explain," Firalod replied. "And to be honest, I do not fully understand it myself, as is befitting my station. But I do believe Illya may be of some help if you take her along."

Lakiva's mouth had formed a tight line, as though he held his anger back with some difficulty, but he did not object.

"One more would not hurt our chances of sneaking in and out," Never said.

Lord Dakan rose. "So be it. I will think upon who to send with you to the camp at Mount Siyapol – an escort you can leave behind if you deem it the best course of action upon reaching the den," he added before Sacha could open her mouth to object, no doubt. "Until then, please seek your rest, as you each have a harrowing path to start on the morrow."

Chapter 20.

Never rose from his bed at the light pouring into his room, a hand slipping beneath the pillow for one of his blades – almost a reflex.

A figure held a raised lamp, rendered indistinct by the brightness.

"Never?"

Sacha's voice.

"I'm awake," he said. His eyes finally adjusted; she wore a cinched tunic and soft pants now, a more casual Vadiya outfit, something he had not seen in many years.

"Good."

He waited, a slow chill creeping across his bare chest. Too bad the embers in his fireplace had grown so low, their glow barely reached the war-like ornaments that sat upon the mantle.

"Never, I want to make something clear – I have not forgiven you."

He raised an eyebrow. "That's what you came in the middle of the night to wake me for?"

"Shut your fool mouth for a moment," she snapped. "I have said this before; I trust your sense of duty. I know you will fight to stop the Svikamet because it is the right thing for Vadiya, for all nations. I know that. And I believe you accept the same from me, that I will do all I can to work together and meet that goal."

"We've gone over this but I will say again, that I'm happy to hear such words."

"You may not enjoy the next ones."

He leant forward with a frown. "Going to tell me that you will kill me when it's all over? I suppose, the moment I land the finishing blow on Dromanev you're planning to slip up behind me with a dagger for my ribs, is that right? You wanted to give me fair warning?"

She swung her arm but he caught her wrist.

Never sighed. "You're right, I deserved to be slapped at the least, because I know you would not be so underhanded – but truly, Sacha, is this your only option?"

"Meaning what?" She did not struggle but nor did he release her.

"We can talk."

"No. We cannot."

"Then don't let me keep you from your rest," Never said as he released her and lay back.

She gave him a short nod and left, taking her light with her. Never let her close the door before he rose, moving to the small stack of wood beside the hearth. He placed a few pieces onto the embers and let them catch hold.

A slow process but worthwhile once the heat returned.

Yet he did not immediately seek his bed... what had she meant to accomplish by reminding him of her promise? Did she fear that his accommodating behaviour was a sign of old feelings? Was *she* rejecting returning fondness of her own? No, that wasn't likely. And she'd always been prideful but the reminder suggested insecurity. It wasn't necessary; he believed she meant to strike him down.

Something else was amiss but for whatever reason she had not been able to reveal anything more.

Either that, or he was reading too much into her visit.

Perhaps it was something more obvious – worry for her people? And why not, it was a dire threat they faced.

Glass exploded.

Never rolled away from the window.

A shadowy figure landed, taking half a step toward the bed before whirling as Never found his feet. Twin blades glinted orange a moment – and then the attacker threw.

Never was already swinging a forearm.

He knocked one blade aside. The second sliced into his ribs. Warm blood flowed down his side and Never grunted as he charged. The assassin leapt back, coming up against the wall, but drawing more blades.

Never swung a fist but the man ducked, then leapt closer – yet Never was ready, he drove his knee up into the fellow's chest with a thud. One blade clattered to the floor. The other bit into his other thigh. Never's leg buckled, but he caught the man's wrist and dragged the assassin down with a thump.

The man's hood fell free, revealing a snarling face – Vadiya, human.

"Bastard."

Never caught the man by the throat and squeezed, just enough to cut off – a large crunch rang out in the room.

The assassin was dead.

The man's face grew slack. Then, only the sound of Never's breathing. For perhaps the only time since his hand had changed, Never cursed the birch which lent it so much strength. Whatever secrets the assassin had held, he now held forever.

"Fool."

Never climbed to his feet and checked on his wounds – the bleeding was slowing but they'd still need to be cared for. He found his pants and stepped into them as footsteps thundered in the hall outside, light bursting in as a pair of Steelhawks appeared.

"Is everything all right here?" one asked.

"Once I get some bandages, yes," Never said.

One man ran off and the first, who'd spoken, entered the room and approached the body. He knelt beside it, tearing open the black shirt. "Svikamet scum."

The tattoo of what seemed to be a blazing sun was revealed.

"That's their symbol?" Odd indeed. Why would the cult send an assassin after him if they wanted him to come to the mountain?

The man stood. "Supposedly it represents their idea of a brighter future, free of military rule."

Never raised an eyebrow. "Something of an exaggeration, there."

"Right," the man said. He moved to the window then and peered out, raising his lamp. Then he drew the curtains and glanced at Never, about to ask something it seemed... but no words followed.

He was staring at Never's chest.

The glow of the five-pointed leaf was clear from where it blinked beneath his skin... only to fade just as quickly.

"What...?"

"I suppose you've heard rumours about the war then, soldier?"

He nodded, eyes a little wide.

"Then consider that just another unbelievable thing you don't have to worry about."

"Ah... I'll do my best... sir."

More footsteps approached; the guard from before, now joined by Father Lakiva and a healer, who set to bandaging Never at once.

"We should move you," Lakiva said. "Just to be safe."

Never lifted his arm for the healer to better access his ribs. "If it allows me to salvage some of this night's sleep then I'm happy to do that."

"I'll have someone organise that room and a search of the grounds," the Steelhawk said as he hurried out.

"And notify Lord Isajan," Lakiva called after.

Once his wounds had been bandaged, Never thanked the man and joined Lakiva by the body. "Does he carry anything of use?" Never asked.

Lakiva hesitated. "I cannot perform any such search; I was merely preparing a prayer for the deceased."

Never started with the outer pockets in the robe but all were empty, as were the hidden pockets within. Nothing inside the man's boots either... and then there was little left to search. No clues as to why, but that was no surprise, truly. Of note, the boots were thinning on the soul and the fellow did seem perhaps a little thin... struck by lean times?

"Nothing," Never said. "Father, let's try that new room, shall we?"

"I need but a moment," he said, bowing his head and speaking softly. "Gather him to your Mighty Halls, God, and allow him..."

The words faded as a trembling page entered to lead Never to another room – it was some distance away, through darkened halls of cold stone, tapestries stirring in draughts, but Lakiva's footsteps were not too distant.

Hopefully it was Lakiva – another attack would be beyond irritating.

"I trust this is suitable," the lad said as he opened the door to reveal a similar lodging to his last, bed, cold fireplace and basin beside a closet. No window, however.

"Of course," Never replied.

"I'll start the fire," he said, darting to the hearth.

Never checked the closet and beneath the bed, but no sign of anyone lurking within the space, by which time Lakiva had rejoined him and also now, the Lord of the keep. Dakan did not appear as though he'd been roused from sleep, sword belted over a black tabard.

"It seems a poor welcome we have offered," he said as he entered.

Lakiva placed Never's pack in the corner.

"It's not your fault, My Lord," Never said. "Besides, I have an idea about who was responsible." Someone with a grudge and someone who had fallen upon hard times.

"Oh?"

"Yes. I believe you'll find the assassin was a Boar." He explained about the confrontation on the stair. "Harstas' sister seemed unhinged enough to try something like this.

I didn't notice a closer family resemblance, so maybe the assassin was a cousin?"

"Hmmm. If this is true, she will be executed at once—"

"My Lord, perhaps imprisonment would be enough."

He frowned. "Is this a request for mercy or do you worry about further attacks?"

"Perhaps both."

"Very well," he said with a slow nod. "Try and rest for what remains of the night. I will post a guard. Until the morrow, then."

Chapter 21.

The road leading from Vitrii up into the hulking mountains was scattered with snow, though it had turned to sleet in the gutters. White graced every surface; the black pines, the undergrowth, the stumps, the road signs and even some stubborn mushrooms. It sparkled beneath the increasingly powerless sun, almost defiant.

From somewhere within the trees came the howl of a wolf and Never stared into the rows of trunks. Of course, he'd not seen the animal but it was a little unusual for wolves to come so close to a city.

"They'll slow us down, you know," Sacha said where she rode beside him, her breath steaming. She glanced over her shoulder to the score of Steelhawks, armour bright. "Instead of three days to the camp, it'll take nearly five now."

Never grinned as he rubbed his hands together for warmth. "Did you want me to send them back to your father? I'm sure he'd like that."

She frowned at him.

"Ah, so you just wanted to vent, I see." He nearly asked her about the previous night but decided against it; she was already in a dark mood. Sweat still beaded on her brow despite the cold – was the vanilla losing its potency? Her visit still played upon his mind, more than the attempted assassination.

"It's not that I don't understand. And his care is better than the indifference when he once focused only on my brothers... but I am impatient, Never. Dromanev and his abominations have killed far too many and we haven't been able to protect the people as I'd wish."

"I'm glad to hear that you seem to care more than you did but we shouldn't rush, either," he said.

"And what does that mean?"

"It means I find this concern for your people more agreeable than your indifference to other nations when we last met."

"That *is* different, to want more for my people."

"How much more does Vadiya need?"

She looked away. "That was his vision – and maybe I believed in *him* more than any particular goal. I would have followed your brother anywhere."

It could have been taken as a touching declaration of love. But to follow so blindly... was it a testament to Snow's power rather than her weakness? Would she have felt the same had she known his true name? Known that Father wanted his son to be the one to *ruin*? Perhaps. But Never steered the conversation away from a topic that would only spoil her mood further. Not to mention his own. "Did you ever get close enough to Dromanev to learn something we can use?"

"I crossed swords with him once; he was fast and strong, even when he appeared mostly human." She shrugged, her gaze on their white surrounds. "But no, not truly. I can only say he is cruel and empty – if you had seen what he left behind in some of the villages."

"Bad?"

She nodded. "One man had obviously not taken to the seed. A villager. His rib cage had grown so much that it burst from his back, encircling his entire torso. The bones had changed too, they were bigger, thicker – they crushed the very life from the poor soul."

"They are taking people, too? It's not just volunteers from the cult?"

"Yes. Some from every town. They had been moving north from the forest and to the sea. They had started east when we picked up their trail. Thankfully for us, the stakolin tend to travel in pairs or alone, save for a few human cultists. My brothers are helping the king focus on the central plains and the south east."

"I should have asked before, but how long has Dromanev been at work?"

Sacha shook her head. "We're not sure. The first sighting of a creature was back in summer – here in the mountains actually. A hamlet near the old iron mine; deserted now. East of where we must travel."

"If we knew how they started, knew *what* it was that set this Dromanev off, it might help. Unless, of course, it was an accident?"

"Perhaps someone led him to the seed."

"You think he has a master?"

"Not until I see otherwise but I want to keep our thinking open." She glanced over at him. "Have you thought about what to do if they already have scores of stakolin?"

He checked on one of his bandages; still holding nicely. "No."

"Wonderful."

"We can worry about that when we learn their numbers but everything hinges on discovering a real weakness. I *can* burn and break them but I'm only one."

"We will find something," she said. "I wonder about the *nekromant*."

Never's horse seemed to flinch at the word, and he gave the mare a calming pat. "What do you know of them? I'd ask Father Lakiva but he doesn't seem too enamoured of the idea."

"Only that they are said to be able to speak to and control the dead. And that they do not need sleep."

"No sleep?"

"The legend says it is a defence against the dead they force to do their bidding – if they sleep, they will be pulled down into the Land of Soot and Ash."

"So, this Illya will be handy for watch duty then."

Sacha shook her head, but he wondered – had there been the faint suggestion of a smile too? He could not tell when she next spoke. "There's a camp not too far ahead; we'll reach it by noon. Let's check with Father Lakiva once more; he might be willing to talk now that he's had some time to grow used to it."

But the priest did not.

When they stopped to eat at the well-established campsite the man would not speak about the *nekromant* despite the way Sacha had glared at the him, but Never chose not to push the priest, and Sacha did not hound him during their meal. Soon enough, they set out again.

He suffered only a twinge of pain while mounting up; his wounds were healing as swiftly as ever.

They rode on without event until evening – where they used another walled camp, this one quite similar to the enclosure in the swamps, though it was just as cold. Never had been about to seek his tent when he saw Sacha scraping vanilla seeds into boiling water.

"Does it still work?" he asked.

She nodded. "For now."

"You're worried about the potency?"

"No, the quantity."

"It would not take me too long to fly back to the city to collect more if you run out."

"Thank you," she said, speaking softly.

Never continued to his tent; he had no doubt his words brought Snow to the forefront of her mind once more, if his brother hadn't been there already. Still, Never refused to let her become one of those creatures.

***

The next few days of travel were similar, climbing the smooth and straight road, stopping at the perfectly placed rest areas and equally well-spaced camps, all fortified. Little changed when it came to the weather or the professionalism of the Steelhawks and despite Sacha's concerns, they made good time.

Yet her sickness seemed to be taking hold once more; when they rode, she still broke into a sweat easily and of an evening, her hands shook when she prepared the tea. And it wasn't the thinning mountain air, something she'd have been used to all her life.

The night before they were due to reach the camp of Steelhawks who'd been posted to watch over the den, Never sat beside her. "I can get more vanilla if you want to try doubling the dose."

"I did that this morning." Her jaw was clenched. "It's not working anymore, we've been missing other ingredients since the beginning."

Never drew a blade – it was the only way... just a drop, maybe it would be enough. And so little... that wouldn't create a new problem surely? The bigger issue would be if she succumbed to the transformation. "Add this." He pricked his finger and let a drop fall into her tea.

"Never?"

"My blood burned away the creature's taint, just like it does other illnesses."

"Are you sure?" Her expression had not changed from determined, angry even, but he saw the fear behind her fierceness.

So unlike her.

But why wouldn't she fear becoming such a thing?

"It's something we can easily increase if one drop isn't enough. Try it."

She nodded, then downed the tea in one gulp.

He waited a moment. "Anything?"

"It's too soon... I'll pay attention."

"Perhaps we should try more tomorrow," he said. "Wake me if you need anything."

She narrowed her eyes at his final words. "I don't need a nursemaid."

"That I know."

Chapter 22.

The military post that had been set to watch the lair of the cult was more highly fortified than the others Never had used thus far, but not actually positioned close enough to see their den – an odd choice, though perhaps it had been placed for its defensive position. It not only blocked the entire highway but stretched out just before a significant narrowing of the trail. The mountain walls rose up in dark stone streaked with granite.

It would work as a good stop gap if the creatures sought to attack the city – there was a wall of stone and a gate of oak fortified by heavy steel bands. Before it, a palisade and small archers' platforms. Most of the two hundred-strong force moving about the camp bore crossbows as part of their equipment and many of them seemed to be First Rangers. Braziers burned at regular intervals too – part of the defence? It seemed somewhat wasteful otherwise, considering the scarcity of dry fuel.

The captain met them in the command tent, which bore the standard of the Isajan family – the red talon. Inside was sparse; a cot, war chest, and a large map set upon a table. The man bowed deeply to Sacha and nodded briefly to Never and Lakiva, a scar running beneath one of his pale blue eyes.

"My Lady; it brings me joy to see you here – I trust it means your father has reconsidered?"

"Rodan." She gripped him by the wrist a moment. "I fear it is not so – unless you thought my score of men were enough for what's up there?"

He growled. "Well, I'd hoped you were just the advance."

"Not yet, we don't have enough information – am I wrong?"

Captain Rodan spread his gauntleted hands. "Part of me agrees."

"And the rest wants to take it to the creatures, right?"

"Exactly."

"Well, let us find a proper weakness first. We're taking Illya into the mountains. When we return, we'll have something."

"I'd welcome that," he said. "How many men can I offer?"

"None."

He frowned. "My Lady?"

"It will be Father Lakiva here and Never – the Winged Hero of Marlosi."

"That's not the name I prefer," Never said.

The captain turned a fairly dour gaze his way. "I thought he'd be taller."

Never grinned. "Maybe if you walked around on your knees for a while, I'd seem bigger." Thus far it had not been too troublesome working with those he ought to have considered enemy, but it seemed Captain Rodan was going to put a stop to that.

Rodan put a hand on his sword hilt. "My Lady, you'd better tell our 'ally' here to watch his mouth."

"Enough!" Sacha snapped. "Both of you. Don't we have enough trouble with the stakolin?"

"Yes, of course, well said," Never replied. "Why doesn't the captain introduce us to Illya?"

The man cleared his throat. "A fine idea. Please, follow me." Rodan led them back into the camp and toward the rear, and then the road, where he turned into the dark trees and began to follow an animal path that wound its way through the dim light.

"Why is she out here?" Sacha asked.

Captain Rodan answered without looking over his shoulder, eyes on the trees, as if searching for a marker. "The men are not at ease when she is near."

"And she chose this?"

"We made her a hut," he said. "She can explain it all better than I, My Lady."

Ahead, a square, box-like room of timber sat between a crowd of trunks. No light appeared from within, no sound either.

"Is she inside?" Never asked.

"She is," Rodan replied. "She rests during the day. I'll let you speak with her, My Lady, please excuse me."

"I believe I will join him," Father Lakiva said.

Never glanced at the man, but Lakiva offered no further explanation. Hardly a good sign; the priest would have to find a way to overcome his prejudice soon enough.

Sacha shrugged as she approached the door. It had been hastily constructed by the looks of it – there were gaps where it met both floor and roof, but it did seem sturdy enough when Sacha knocked. "Illya?"

A moment of silence before a young woman's voice answered. "Yes?"

"My father, Lord Isajan and High Priest Firalod sent us here to deal with the stakolin and they believe you can help. We wanted to meet you."

"Please, come in."

Sacha opened the door and it seemed she met some resistance at a heavy black cloth that covered the doorway. A rectangle of light revealed a cot up against the wall, blankets a little rumpled, and barrel of water beside the narrow bed – but no sign of Illya... he blinked. She stood opposite the bed, facing the wall. "Sorry to appear rude, I need to prepare my eyes."

Pale hair ran halfway down her back, covering equally pale shoulders – her white vest did not appear to be cloth or leather but fur... or feathers? After a little longer standing and breathing, she turned.

She squinted at first, and it seemed she was a young woman with delicate features but it was her eyes that he noticed first: they were a bright blue, seeming stronger due to the twin tattoos that ran from her eyelids down her cheek – black feathers.

"I am Illya," she said with a faint smile. "And you must be Lady Sacha of the Isajan Family, and you, Never the Amouni."

"You know us?" Sacha asked, her expression a touch unnerved.

"I do."

"I hope we haven't caused you undue pain?" Never asked.

"Captain Rodan said you were resting." How she knew about him was something that could wait a moment, for something about her good-natured acceptance of having to remain so isolated added to the sadness of the situation. He knew nothing of the *nekromant* but it was obvious there'd be an inherent loneliness, if they were so few.

Illya waved a hand. "It is no trouble; I am glad to speak with you both."

"High Priest Firalod said that so far, you haven't been able to learn anything," Sacha said.

She shook her head. "The occasional stakolin that has approached tended to withdraw rather than attack and the few patrols they took me on during the night yielded nothing. To truly help, I suspect I'll need to enter the caves. I have considered it, but I sensed you coming and thought I should wait."

"You would have gone alone?" Never asked.

"I have nothing to fear from them."

"Because of your powers?"

"Partially, but also because after living so close and for so long to the Slumbering Pillars, I do not need to shy away from my fate; after all, it is everyone's fate. Even Amouni, in time, must pass from this world."

Again, Never forced himself to set aside his curiosity – though the suggestion that he might live a long, long life was probably more disconcerting than comforting. "We hoped you'd come with us actually. If we ambushed a creature, would you be able to communicate with it?"

"Yes."

"You seem confident," Sacha said.

"They were once human – though that is no requirement.

I can speak to animals too, if needed."

"Do the animals here talk?" Sacha asked.

"I came across a wolf who believed the stakolin were searching for something in the mountains – the cult have been in and out of all the caves they find."

"What could they seek in Mount Siyapol?" Never asked.

Sacha shook her head. "I don't know. It's always been a wild place – few choose to live much higher than where we stand. The winters are too vicious."

"I have a theory," Illya said. "They seek the Temple of Oleksan."

Sacha gasped.

"Who?" Once again, Never found himself a little behind – his knowledge of Vadiya history was in no way all-encompassing.

"The Burnished King, Oleksan he was named," Sacha replied. "He is described as a tyrant who forced the ancient Vadiyem kingdoms into unity – only to later turn upon those around him."

"He launched a war of annihilation against his own people," Illya added, "that was only halted when they called for aid from the forebears of those who are called Hanik today. It was said to be over fifteen hundred years ago now."

"And why would they seek his temple?" Never asked.

"Obviously, to Resurrect the Burnished King."

Never exhaled. "Because he will lead them on a new rampage with some dread power?"

Illya nodded.

"Supposedly King Oleksan bore a weapon called the *kirinth-dela* – the Blight Hammer, in the modern tongue,"

Sacha said. "If you believe the legends, it cast decay and pestilence wherever it struck."

"If there is even a remote chance of this being true, we need to tell your father and the High Priest," Never said.

"I have already made a report of my suspicions to Captain Rodan. I doubt he found them credible," she said.

"Hmmm." Something else weighed upon his mind – the bait that he had willingly took; was that the other purpose? Dromanev needed Amouni blood to raise the Burnished King?

And whether Never went charging in or if he tried to sneak into the lair as planned, he'd be giving the cult exactly what they sought.

Chapter 23.

"I harbour the same concern, Never," the *nekromant* said into the quiet that followed her last announcement. Her expression was quite serene, however, and the vivid blue of her eyes seemed to draw the light within, a kind of odd hope... or so it seemed.

"That they want to use you?" Never said.

"Yes, though I do not know if they are aware of my presence."

Sacha held up a hand. "Wait a moment. Are you both saying that Svikamet believes they can find the temple, find Oleksan and then use you two to bring the Burnished King back to life, where he will lead them in some unholy war?"

"Not to life," Illya said. "But to a walking death. It is possible, I suppose, that I could bring him back, after a fashion."

"We will stop Dromanev well before that becomes a problem," Never said. Again, being drawn to the mountain was only bait if the cult's plan worked. It was no clever ploy if they all died – something he would ensure happened.

"Right," Sacha said. "Let's deal with our living foes."

Illya inclined her head. "Of course, Lady Sacha. I trust you wouldn't be offended if I were to continue to rest here until evening?"

"Not at all," she said, and Never smiled at the *nekromant* before following Sacha out into the forest. He closed the door and caught up to Sacha, who was striding along the cold dirt.

"What did you make of her, Never?"

"I've no reason to doubt her, if that's what you're asking. I suspect she can do what she claims and so we need a stakolin corpse."

"And the story about the Burnished King?"

"Well... I've seen enough unbelievable things that I wouldn't discount it outright. I mean, I'm an impossibility myself – so why not King Oleksan?"

Her hand strayed to her weapon as she answered. "Then we do as you say. We stop Dromanev before he can get his hands on you."

"I'm happy to hear you don't think my coming here is a risk," he said as they reached the road and started for the camp.

She shrugged. "It is. But what move is totally without risk? We have to act and you are our best chance. Anyway, I want to see the sentry post. Feel like taking a walk?"

"You don't want to ride?"

"I don't think it's so far – come on."

Sacha strode through the camp, sending one of her men to inform Captain Rodan of her plan, then had the men open the gates. The sergeant hesitated but could not refuse, and Sacha waved off his offer to send some men along. "We won't be long."

A field of stakes formed a palisade, ends fired, providing a difficult path to the wall – no doubt a measure to slow rather than stop the creatures, and thus provide easy targets. Hopefully it would be enough if an attack came. The road lead directly through the narrowing of the mountain pass, long shadows covering the stone.

"How is your fever?" Never asked once they'd cleared the pass.

"The blood helped," she said, though she was breathing a little hard.

"But?"

"But it has not fully gone... I feel it within me somehow. It's fighting to stay."

"We'll double the dose tonight," Never said.

"If you say so."

He nodded. "I won't let it happen to you."

She stopped then, her expression suddenly wary. "I hope that isn't an attempt to manipulate me, Never."

He resumed walking.

"Well?"

"What do you want me to say, Sacha?" he replied, unable to prevent a long sigh escaping. "Don't tell me that you believe in my sense of duty again and again, and then imply that I want to stop you becoming a creature just to save my own skin." He didn't add that despite her far superior swordsmanship, she would have no chance of striking him down.

She caught his arm. "Wait – you're right."

Once more, he did not ask her what was truly amiss

– or, attempt to convey understanding, if her distrust was fuelled by fear. She had every right to be unsettled with the poison of the cult within her. But she wasn't going to accept sympathy. "Then let's focus on the lair, right?"

"Yes."

The highway continued climbing; it was a little narrower now, joined occasionally by paths that led around the peaks or into stands of trees, only half with signs. Fewer merchants bringing their wares down to the city here, no doubt.

Before too long, a pair of Steelhawks stepped from the trees, weapons raised – though they lowered them upon recognising Sacha.

"My Lady?" The bearded one went to one knee before rising again.

"Can you take us up? We want to see the lair."

"Of course, follow me." He led them into the trees, leaving his fellow behind, and not far within, they came to a broad tree bearing a ladder of chain links. It stretched up the trunk, soon lost between the branches. "Vin is up there but there's room for three if you squeeze in."

Sacha thanked him as she started up. Never gave her a moment before following, shaking his head when grains of dirt from her boots rained down on him. He climbed on. The pine needles bore little scent in the cold – either that or his nose had given up as the chill to the air grew, but when he joined Sacha and another Steelhawk upon a reinforced platform, he was rewarded with a fine vantage.

The tree was obviously one of the tallest in the area, and it provided a clear view of the forest, waves of gently swaying pines and beyond to the east, an opening in the rock face of Mount Siyapol, the jagged peaks tipped with snow.

"That is their lair?" Sacha asked.

He nodded. "There's been no movement today, My Lady."

"When was the last time they left?" she asked.

"Around evening, same time every day. Sometimes it's the cultists with one of the creatures, but always a creature; it leaves to hunt for meat." He frowned. "We hear the animals."

"Have you tried to kill one for Illya to read?" Never asked.

"Only twice – neither time went well, so the captain has been trying to come up with something else."

Never grinned. "Well, you're in luck because we're the something else."

Chapter 24.

"Satisfied?"

Never raised the globe of crimson-fire in his hand, flaring it enough to light the gathered faces – many slack with shock, yet a few were almost snarling in... fear or hatred? No matter. The most important face was that of Rodan, and his sceptical expression had darkened to grudging acquiescence.

"I do concede that between you and Father Lakiva, you ought to be able to protect My Lady."

Never let the flame fade away to a small tongue and shadows fell over the camp once more, save for the light cast by the slumbering braziers.

"And Illya," Sacha said, glancing to the edge of the camp where a pale figure stood in silence. Then she folded her arms, pointing a gauntleted finger at the man. "And none of that ought to have been necessary, Captain. Your insubordination has been noted."

He knelt. "Forgive me, My Lady, but your father would have me killed were I to fail to protect you."

"That is for Never to worry about – you need to protect

the city. Stay vigilant while we are gone." Sacha raised her voice. "Understood?"

"Yes, My Lady," the crowd replied.

Sacha set off through the gate at a jog. Never followed, Lakiva keeping pace beside him, mighty hammer still strapped to his back. "Have you come to terms with Illya?" Never asked as they wove through the palisade. Presumably the young woman trailed them, as she'd said she would, but he did not see her when he glanced back at the camp and the watching soldiers.

"I am trying."

"Good. We cannot afford to make any mistakes tonight."

The priest nodded but added nothing more and they travelled in silence the rest of the way to the sentry post. From there, it was time to leave the highway, moving onto an animal trail that led toward the lair. At first, the stony path hugged the mountain walls but it was soon swallowed up by the pines, the needles almost hissing beneath the passage of their feet.

When they had climbed to a point that was adjacent from the black cave opening, Sacha whispered for a halt where she crouched beside a twin-trunk. "Now we wait."

"Do we know for how long?" Lakiva asked.

"Vin said before midnight?" Never replied. "Can you feel them?"

"No... it's as if something is in the lair but it is so... generalised that I cannot pinpoint anything with the Echo."

"One of the stakolin has already left the lair," a voice added – Illya; she stood nearby, her pale figure slender in the shadows, yet her blue eyes were as vivid as ever. Father

Lakiva did not turn to look at her.

"How can you be sure?" Sacha asked.

"They have a particular scent – though that is not a very accurate description."

"Nearby?" Never asked.

"No, but heading back toward a group of cult members. It is some distance away yet."

"Let's take a look," Sacha said. "Lead the way."

This time they followed the white shape of Illya as she flitted from tree to tree, not precisely running nor floating... yet she was no ghost, of that Never was sure. Now, at night, the sense of her otherworldliness was strong. Did her powers also come from a splintered line of Amouni, or had the *nekromant* always walked the lands?

At a point west of the lair, Illya slowed, eventually stopping before a cluster of trunks. Murmuring voices and dragging sounds were audible. "Beyond is their harvest."

"Harvest?" Never asked.

"The bodies of animals for meat."

Sacha signalled for them to approach at a crawl. Never did so, using his elbows and knees with some care, coming to a stop at the edge of a sloping depression. Shadowy figures moved within, lifting and carrying darker shapes across the clearing. The sharp scent of blood was clear – and the longer he stared down at them, the easier it was to discern between deer, rabbit, wolf and even what seemed to be... portions of a bear?

The cultists were nearly finished collecting what they had, setting out in pairs or singly. Yet one figure remained behind. Perhaps waiting for the creature?

Never whispered. "I'm going to replace him. When

I'm done, circle around. We'll flank the creature when I strike."Sacha nodded and Lakiva did too, muttering a prayer to the Vadiya god. Never glanced back to Illya. She nodded, presumably she would be able to help with the actual killing. Perhaps no surprise there, but at least she was ready.

Yet he waited a little longer, giving the line of cultists more time to make some distance, before drawing a knife.

He paused, a single breath to steady himself and then – rose and threw in one motion. The steel flew down into the depression and thudded into the man's back. He pitched forward without a sound.

"Nice to start with some luck," he said.

"Hurry; it approaches," Illya said.

Never leapt down, sliding on needles and running across the floor. There, he grabbed the dead man's arms and hauled, grunting with effort. Once he had the man concealed behind a tree, he tore the fellow's robe and pulled it across his body, raising the hood.

Then he stood in the centre of the clearing.

The crunching of branches echoed from afar. Never sliced into both palms, letting the blood pool slowly. The creature's charging grew larger in the night. "Come closer, you monster," Never whispered.

Taginus had not been easy to take down but this battle would be different – they had surprise on their side. So long as no-one from the cave noticed the struggle... the cultists would have returned by now. Nevertheless, it had to be quick.

Yellow eyes soon approached from between the trees, striding forward. The figure was tall and hulking, the shape somewhat unclear due to the pair of deer, one slung over each shoulder. Was the face somehow familiar, even in the cloak of darkness?

The eyes lit enough facial features... it was the stakolin from the bridge... Cevana?

The creature dumped both animals down with barely a glance, turning as if to complete another hunt.

Never let the crimson-fire burst free in twin streams.

Wild shadows leapt, turning the trunks red as flame roared across the clearing. It splashed across the creature's back. Earth sprayed from clawed feet as it wheeled in shock. The eyes blazed now – in glee, it seemed. "Amouni!"

It shot forward.

Never charged.

Light flashed from the side, Lakiva and his nimbus of holy power. He closed with the creature and swung his hammer. The stakolin twisted, catching the blow with a roar. Steel flashed from its opposite side as Sacha had lunged forth. It seemed she'd traded her long sword for a rapier.

Her blade sunk into the flesh – she'd aimed for a leg joint, and unlike a regular slash or overhand blow, her blade sunk a little deeper than Never had expected. Cevana lashed out with his free hand but Sacha had already ducked away.

Never crashed into the beast, driving his burning birch hand into the thing's chest. Bone crunched and a scream rose – this one quite human; and despite the distorted nature of the sound... somewhat feminine. Cevana was a woman.

His surprise was fleeting.

Never skipped back, talons grazing his arm as he did.

Cevana pushed Lakiva aside as she stumbled forward.

The priest hit the loam hard, light faltering, but he found his feet quickly. Cevana's breaths were haggard. "You are finished," Never said as he approached one more. "You will not slaughter another innocent."

Cevana gurgled something but it was unintelligible.

A hacking cough followed – blood splashing across the needles. She fell to her knees then. Never let another burst of crimson-fire shoot forth, though he narrowed it, thin like the blade of a chisel – and focused it all on the creature's head. Steam rose and Cevana thrashed.

A shout resounded from behind her.

Father Lakiva leapt forth, swinging a mighty overhand blow.

Light flashed and thunder boomed – and something splattered across the clearing. Blinding white faded as Never blinked. When he could see again, Lakiva stood over a broken shape, the entire back and shoulder of the stakolin broken.

Flesh and blood had splattered around the corpse, some of it landing at Never's feet but Lakiva was spotless, the nimbus, which even now faded, had protected him.

A white figure flashed forward.

Illya knelt beside Cevana. "I must be swift," she said.

"Are others coming?" he asked.

"No – I just don't know how much time I have; it may differ with a stakolin."

A blue glow spread from the *nekromant*'s face as she began to speak. Each word was firm, precise – and like nothing Never had ever heard. It was not like Vadiya, modern or ancient, nor Amouni either; it seemed aside from human language. More general somehow... as though conveying much through fewer sounds. It hardly made sense but why would it? He was no necromancer.

Illya repeated the words twice more and then exhaled.

She closed her eyes, casting darkness – and then opened them again; now her irises had turned black and only Lakiva's nimbus lit the clearing.

Cevana stirred.

The battered head began to turn. Slowly, it twisted up to face Illya – and the creature's eyes glowed faintly blue now. The half of the body that was whole twitched again, leg thrashing. Illya brought her hands together and Cevana's corpse grew still.

Then, Illya opened her mouth – but no sound followed. When she stopped, Cevana spoke... yet it was Illya's voice that answered. Again, the words were unfamiliar. Never focused on them as the conversation continued but still the meaning eluded him, even with his Amouni gift for language.

The conversation continued in the same pattern a little longer until the light in Cevana's eyes wavered... tears were streaming forth. Never frowned. Gods, what did it mean? Never glanced at Illya but her pale face remained dry.

And then the young woman spread her hands apart and spoke a single word.

Cevana's head fell to the side.

The light was gone – and then Illya was shuddering as she too, toppled to the torn earth. Never caught her. She was breathing but her eyes were closed. "Lakiva, Sacha, we need to get out of here," he said, glancing around the clearing.

At the limit of Father Lakiva's light, Sacha lay unmoving beyond the creature's body.

Chapter 25.

"Carry her," Never told the priest, then ran to Sacha.

He knelt by her side; she, too, was breathing but her chest rose and fell in an uneven pattern. Blood covered part of her head, face and side... but it was not hers for he felt no wounds when he checked.

It belonged to the stakolin.

The spray of blood from Lakiva's killing blow must have caught her and now, somehow, it was having a far more accelerated effect on Sacha. Was it because she was already fighting off the *disrytha* or was it due to something else? Was it simply too strong?

"Hurry," Never said, and scooped Sacha into his arms. He dashed across the clearing, climbing the slope with clenched teeth. If the cultists had heard the fight, if they'd seen the crimson-fire or Lakiva's holy light...

"Do you know the way?" Lakiva asked. If the priest was unwilling to touch the woman he'd barely been able to look upon thus far, he showed no signs of it. His brows were drawn together in determination.

"Distance first," Never said. "And stop glowing."

The nimbus faded away and together they slowed but continued on, racing from clearing to clearing, aided by the newly-risen moon. Yet just as often, they had to stop and detour; once due to fallen trunk and several times after the trail led only to a wall of undergrowth. When they took a moment to rest, Never would place Sacha down carefully then check upon their back trail.

Each time, no signs of pursuit.

The night wore on and Never found himself calling a halt more frequently; checking on Sacha more often. When her breathing worsened to rasping he found a hollow ringed by trees with low-hanging branches and stopped.

"I need to do something," he said. "Watch for pursuit, Father."

Lakiva placed Illya down with a nod, moving a little way along the back trail. "All clear."

"Good." Never knelt to arrange Sacha in a half-sitting position against a trunk. Her eyes were screwed shut, yet she did not respond when he called her name. Her chest rose and fell in an erratic rhythm even as he drew his blade.

"Gods, not again." His own heart thumped – had he waited too long? Losing her wasn't an option.

Focus!

He sliced into his palm, cutting a little deeper than he'd intended. Blood welled, overflowing to drip to the needles. He cupped his hand and with the other, tilted her head. Then, he pulled her jaw open. "Hold on, Sacha." She groaned but he poured the blood within anyway and closed her mouth. She swallowed – only to cough half his blood back onto his hand.

Never swore; he had no time to prepare his blood with water or tea, no time to try and wake her, and so he let more blood flow and again she swallowed, loosing enough that he tried a third time...

And finally her breathing eased.

Her shoulders slumped back against the bark and her head fell to the side, frown lines easing. They did not disappear, but it was better than before.

"Never?" Lakiva asked.

"It's working." Yet, how well? He'd shared more with Muka back in Kiymako, without truly knowing what effect it had on the man. What would Amouni blood do to Sacha? Improve her healing? Something else?

So long as it saved her.

A hand came to rest on his shoulder. Illya stood beside him. "She is going to recover, for now."

"For now?" he didn't bother asking how she knew.

"I fear the taint may be harder to shake off than these first measures."

Whatever it took. He nodded before looking up to the *nekromant*. "Are you well?"

"Yes, I do not usually react so. The true force of the stakolin was unexpected; it is not unlike a wrestling contest in some ways." She looked across to Lakiva. "Thank you for carrying me, Father Lakiva."

"You are welcome," he said. He did not join them yet his voice was hardly laced with ice, either.

"You spoke in a language I have not heard before," Never said.

"Yes. I must make the dead speak. We call it the Prose of the Dead and it is not taught to those beyond the Clan but even this much may be neglecting my duties to protect it from dissemination, considering your heritage," she said.

He raised an eyebrow. "I may learn languages swiftly now but that was like... nothing and everything at the same time."

"That eases my worry," she replied with a small smile. "As for what Cevana said... it was her regret which came through most strongly. She was the only woman, so far, to have a successful transformation."

"She told you that?"

"Yes. Unlike many others, despite the initial resistance, and the brute force of her Ending, she was willing to speak."

"She shared a weakness?"

"Yes. The stakolin are rendered vulnerable to impurities in the air after ingesting the seed – something about their lungs; I could not hold her long enough for any more."

Finally. "No need to apologise. We have something now."

"It seems slight."

"It'll simply take a bit of planning for when we return," Never said as he checked on Sacha; she was still breathing evenly. He lifted her. "Time to move on, I think."

Illya nodded and Lakiva joined Never as he led them from the hollow, heading in a direction that he felt was close to the highway, though he could not be certain. At a crossroads where two animal trails met, he hesitated.

"I can lead if you wish?" Illya said.

"Please."

She darted ahead, moving far more fleet of foot than seemed natural and he adjusted the weight of Sacha in his arms before starting after her.

The *nekromant* soon had them back on the road, and it was pleasing to note he'd been travelling in approximately the correct direction. And while Never and Lakiva took the road, Illya ran on a parallel path within the tree line until they approached the palisade.

"Please call upon me if you need me again," she told them, waiting within the trees. "I'll follow when the camp has quietened down after your return."

"I'm sure the captain would—"

"Then you would be wrong, Amouni," she said, a touch of sadness in her voice. "Please, focus on Lady Sacha now."

Behind him, Lakiva was calling to the sentries from the palisade. Never glanced down to the woman he carried. Blessedly, her breathing was still calm enough and there did not seem to be any sweat on her brow – though the sharp chill of the night would not have permitted much. "We owe you a debt, Illya."

"Thank you." She smiled and backed into the shadows.

Chapter 26.

Never woke to the cry of a horn.

Bright sunlight pushed against the pale blue of his tent though it seemed nothing else was beyond – no thunder of feet or cries of alarm. Had he dreamt the call?

A second blast rang across the camp.

He threw the layers of blankets aside and jammed his feet into his boots. Then, he leapt from the tent and into the cold air, blinking against the sun. Soldiers left smoking fires to run for the gates, weapons in hand.

Never joined them, leaping over a fallen pack, and charged to where one of the sentries was calling for Captain Rodan. The man was already climbing to the platform. The press of Steelhawks, some only half in armour, was too great to pass. Never muttered a curse before glancing over his shoulder – no-one stood too close, good.

His wings burst free and he leapt into the air amid shouts of shock.

He climbed quickly, then glided to land atop the gate. From nearby, more gasping from the sentries and those below, but Never glared beyond the palisade. One of the blue-skinned stakolin stood watching the camp, the crumpled form of a human at its feet.

"It hasn't moved since it arrived," a sentry said.

Captain Rodan did not answer.

But the creature did move now – it straightened, twisting its torso, seemingly to face Never, then turned and strode away, quickly lost from sight. Had it been waiting for him? Who was the man or woman on the road? It didn't seem like an attack.

No, a trap was more likely.

Still...

"I'll see what it has done," he called to Rodan, then leapt into the air once more, not waiting for an answer.

He beat his wings over sharpened spikes and then swooped along shadowed stone, tilting his wings so he shot up into the air before breaking free of the pass. Below, no movement, just the small shape of the creature's victim. Never glided over the trees on either side of the highway a moment, narrowing his eyes but again, couldn't penetrate the canopy. The stakolin either lurked within or was already heading back to its lair.

Had the advance scouts seen it? He would check on them – but first, Never circled lower and when he neared the road, he beat his wings and landed in a crouch, cutting his palm as he drew a blade.

Crimson-fire blossomed.

Yet no-one burst from the trees. Never replaced his blade but did not let the flame die away just yet. He approached the motionless body – it, too, might have been part of the trap, yet when he nudged the cloaked shape with his foot, nothing happened. More, the slight movement revealed blood on the paved road.

Never snapped his hand shut as his own blood resonated with the body below.

He reached out to roll the poor man over, a villager by what remained of his clothes, revealing sightless eyes and a slack expression, skin blue with cold, blue with death. Yet a message had been carved into his naked chest, letters vivid in black blood, now mostly dried.

"The boy dies at midnight."

Never clenched his other fist.

The message was simple enough – and effective, since Never would be going directly to the lair now. "Hold on, Temilo."

Never waved to the camp and the gates swung open to reveal half a dozen Hawks, led by Captain Rodan and his rather furious expression. "What are you thinking?" the man shouted as he neared.

"It's a message for me," Never replied.

Rodan's eyes flashed. "You can't risk your life like that, fool – we're depending on you, or have you forgotten?"

"I have to move on the lair tonight," he said. "It's time to do exactly what I have come here to do."

The officer exhaled. "Fine. But we need more time to perfect your idea and Lady Sacha will not appreciate being left behind."

"No, I'll need both her and Father Lakiva."

"Very well, but—"

"And you should double the sentry post – if they're alive," Never said. "I'm going to check on them."

He took a running leap and climbed swiftly, treetops

passing below as he headed for the sentry post. It did not take long to reach, and by the startled wave he received from the man, nothing had gone amiss.

"He... ah, must have slipped past us somehow... My Lord," Vin said.

"No need for any of that."

"So... it's true, then. You're that Winged Hero."

Never shrugged. "I'm winged, that much is true."

Relief passed over the sentry's face. "I hadn't truly believed but seeing you now, I'm actually starting to feel hope."

"Good. Keep a hold of that," Never said as he leapt back into the sky. "The captain is sending more men here."

"Right," the soldier called.

Never flew back toward the camp now, its haze of smoke from campfires easy to spot where it drifted up from behind one of the peaks. Yet as he dropped to swoop between the pass, he lost sight of it.

By then, the wall was within sight and he skimmed over it before wheeling to thump down to the hard earth before Sacha and Lakiva, who were waiting for him at the captain's pavilion. Sacha had her hands on her hips and Father Lakiva bore a softer expression, one bordering on awe.

Which was somehow more disconcerting than a disapproving reaction; adulation was hardly something he craved.

Sacha, at least, looked well – her colour seemed as it should and she wore her armour and weapons. Which suggested that his blood had done its trick. A blessing... but just how deeply would it change her? And had it dealt with the taint of the stakolin?

"What happened?" she asked. "My men are saying you flew out to confront one of the stakolin."

He shook his head. "It didn't wait for me but left a message on a body of a villager – we have to stop them before midnight."

"Temilo?"

He nodded. "I don't want to say it... but he may already be dead. They've already succeeded in bringing me here."

"No," Sacha said. "Temilo is always right, if he told you they were telling the truth back at the bridge then that's that."

"I hope that's still true," Never said. Did the boy's gift extend to possible changes of mind? Or was his gift claiming that the cult members would *not* change their minds? The fellow who'd given the demand may have only been a lackey or a second. Dromanev might have had other plans.

Whatever the specifics of the gift, it didn't mean giving up was an option.

"I am." Sacha gestured to the large tent. "Inside, I want you to tell me more about your idea for slowing those creatures down."

"I told her what happened," Father Lakiva said, slowing his steps.

Never nodded. "Good, that saves me doing it."

"Is she going to be the same?" he asked.

"Yes," Never replied. "If there's a change, it will be for the better."

"So it should be," Sacha called from within the tent.

Inside, she was already pacing.

"Want me to explain what I've had Rodan and your men

working on since we returned? I'd show you but I don't know if they're ready. It's not very sophisticated."

She waved a hand. "Tell me."

"All right. Once Illya mentioned that their lungs were vulnerable I realised we could slow them down with something in powder form – your men are working on transforming crossbows to shoot something that will burst. Then, the stakolin breathe in whatever we have. Personally, I'm hoping it kills but I'd settle for at least slowing them down. If they're having trouble breathing, they won't be the same threat."

Sacha chuckled. "Could it be that easy?"

"Only if it works," Never said.

"It might not be so far-fetched. When we were chasing them... some avoided the wind because it tended to bring dust. I don't think any ever just collapsed but there was one hunt where we didn't lose as many men."

"Winter in the mountains is hardly a dust-prone time," Lakiva added. "I don't know about the interior of the caves, though."

"Ideally, we'd be hitting them with some sort of poison," Never said. "Anything in large supply – I'll collect it from the city or the forest, wherever."

"Are people already searching?" Sacha asked.

"Rodan was going to send people into the woods last night."

"What sort of poison?" Father Lakiva asked. "Aren't we then just as vulnerable?"

"That's our biggest problem so far," Never admitted.

"It's not our only weapon," Sacha said. "You two made short work of the creature we took down."

"Hmmm." Lakiva did not seem convinced.

"At least we know, so long as you have called the Holy Light, you will not be changed by the stakolin's blood – you deflected it after the killing blow." He looked to Sacha. "And you're probably safe now too, having ingested enough of *my* blood."

"I hope that is true," she said.

"It is not dissimilar, is it?" Lakiva asked.

"The use of blood?"

"Yes. The stakolin must bear some relation to Amouni."

"I would not be surprised," Never said. The possible link had only receded to the back of his mind for now; it took little for it to return to the fore. "And more – I would be saddened."

Captain Rodan entered. He tossed his sword onto the cot and went to the chest, where he withdrew a bottle of whiskey and took a long drink before joining them. "We all know it is a trap."

"We do," Sacha said.

"We don't need to wait to spring it, however," Never added.

The captain shook his head but only took another drink. "Moki thinks she has made some adjustments. She wants to show you all."

"Good work, Captain," Sacha said. "Lead the way."

Outside, the soldier stood with a crossbow in one hand and a small pouch in the palm of her other. It had been tied with a draw string but the fabric was of a thinner cloth. The crossbow had been altered. It now featured a small leather cup attached to the string where, presumably, the pouch would rest.

"It's just dirt inside a scrap of an old cloak, My Lady," the grinning woman said as she set the pouch and lifted the weapon, pointing it at a tree at the edge of the camp. She raised her voice in warning then pulled the trigger. The arms snapped and the pouch shot across the camp, smashing against the trunk in a puff of dust. Moki's smiled widened and she blinked for a moment, heaving a sigh. Deep lines rested beneath her eyes – she'd obviously worked through the night. "It's a relief to see it work both times. Well, its range is obviously far less than with a bolt but I've managed to make three already."

"This is impressive work, Moki," Sacha said, accepting the weapon and turning it over in her hands.

Moki went to one knee. "It's my honour, Lady."

Sacha shook her head with a faint smile. "No need for that."

The soldier stood. "I guess all you have to do now is figure out what to put inside."

"There's plenty of noxious weeds around but we can hardly dry and crush enough into a fine powder before midnight," the captain said.

"Whatever we use, I trust you also have something in mind to protect us?" Father Lakiva said.

Moki spread her hands. "Well, for now maybe just cover your mouth and nose with wet kerchiefs?"

"Better than nothing, right?" Never said, slapping the priest on the shoulder.

"But the problem of a suitable powder remains," Sacha said.

"I can leave and return to Vitrii before nightfall if we can reach any nearby river soon," Never said.

"If we're attacked, I don't want to you so far away," the captain said, a certain amount of grudging respect in his voice.

"Wait." Lakiva broke into a jog, heading for the woods at the rear of the camp. "He might not have to."

"Father?"

Never followed, joined by the others, where they caught up with the priest as he climbed a rocky slope beneath the pines. "Here!" He gestured to his feet.

Or, more specifically, the greens, browns, yellows and red of the undergrowth – a vine-like plant that crept across and around the snowy stones. Three leaves on the stems...

Poison ivy.

Chapter 27.

Never focused a stream of crimson-fire into the pit that had been dug in the centre of the camp – steam and faint smoke rose, but the damp poison-ivy and branches were as nothing before his blood. It burned hot enough that the fumes were light; the men approaching were not harmed when they threw their loads in – though most did not stray too near.

The more they brought, the more he burnt.

He took time to stop for food and water but after a good long while, longer than he'd expected he could last, it was time to stop. As to whether it would be enough, he couldn't be sure but it was worth trying. Once the fire burned out, the ash could be collected and then they'd have their weapon.

The difficult part now lay ahead.

And in case of the nest being overflowing with cultists and stakolin, Captain Rodan and his Hawks were going to continue producing the ash. However, something told Never that would not be the case – the cultists did not have enough stakolin to launch a major attack, else they would have done so already.

Whoever waited within the caves would be trouble enough... but the true fear he bore was for Temilo.

"Rest, Never," Sacha said as she approached. The afternoon sun gleamed on her armour, she was more heavily armed now; wearing a modified crossbow along with her rapier and daggers.

"Think that will be enough for now?"

"I want to find Temilo already – we can't carry too much of the ash anyway."

Never let the stream die. "What about Lakiva?"

"Finishing his prayers as we speak."

"And Rodan?"

She sighed. "He wants to send men with us and he's not happy. Not that he can stop us, but I explained that we'd return if they are too many."

"Good." Stealth was the best approach. "Have you seen Illya?"

"No. And I don't think we should yet – let's save it for when we return. I don't want her to get the wrong idea, and think she should come along."

He nodded. "No point delivering both her *and* me in the same visit, right?"

"It's the logical thing to do."

"Meaning you believe the story about the Burnished King?"

"I believe he was a figure from our history. Whether Illya is right about the Svikamet's goal... I don't know. But his kingdom was supposedly here in the south. And there are plenty of other hidden places the cult could have chosen to make their base."

"Then we have two goals," Never said.

"Right. Go gather whatever you're taking – we'll give the ash a little time to cool and then I want to get moving. I don't know how deep their lair will run."

"Good idea." Never headed for his tent and spent a little time preparing water and other supplies – mostly for light – but also took time to eat several helpings of cold meat, bread and cheese. Then he checked his blades, sharpening one before visiting the sentries on the gate – no sign of an attack, which did seem unlikely. Yet the need to keep moving grew.

And doing absolutely nothing would only make it worse.

He gave Sacha another dose of his blood and even took a short flight to scout the surrounding woods but again, found nothing.

Finally, it was time to leave.

Moki had loaded them up with several pouches of ash each, along with the three crossbows. Captain Rodan offered horses, but no more swords, seemingly taking whatever Sacha had said to heart. "God watch over you all," the officer said.

She accepted the mounts and so it was at a swift pace they climbed beyond the palisade, racing the afternoon sun up the mountain. At the sentry post, no reports of movement from the cult – human or stakolin.

Sacha slowed her horse when they started up the final rise, where the cave mouth waited some ways off the road. "Do you sense anything?" she asked Lakiva.

"Nothing close," he said. "I don't know how well I would

be able to sense the stakolin but humans will be no problem."

"So be it," Sacha said. She dismounted, lifted her pack free then gave her mount a slap on the rump, sending it back toward the camp. Never did the same while Lakiva wrestled with his crossbow and war hammer. Maybe it was cruel, leaving them vulnerable to any wolves... but tying them near the lair would only guarantee they were eaten.

"I want to propose something in there," he said. "I lead, Sacha carries her crossbow and Lakiva I want you with a torch."

"The holy light would illuminate much," he said.

"Can you keep it up indefinitely? We don't know how long we'll be in there."

"Actually, no."

"Fine with me," Sacha said as she stepped from the road and into the clearing before the cave. "Let's find Temilo."

The opening had obviously been expanded; rubble still surrounded the entry, some of it splattered with blood... hopefully most of it animal rather than human. Within, a sharp slope led down toward a flickering light. It seemed some distance away and offered no guarantee the entire passage would be lit.

Never paused to listen before stepping within. Nothing. Which provided nothing, of course. He drew a blade and made a thin incision in his finger, letting the spot of blood well up but did not press harder. It was enough to let the crimson-fire free but not so much that it would come anywhere near slicking his hands.

He started down, glancing at the rough-hewn walls as he did; a mix of tool marks and natural protrusions or dips. No tunnels led off the main passage, and when the floor evened out it was near the light – a lamp set in the wall.

But no sign of any life. A few animal bones, perhaps rabbit, had been thrown against the wall but nothing else was of note.

"Dromanev will want us to go deeper before they try anything," Never said as he continued on. The passage soon came to another slope, this one cut with stairs.

Now they travelled deeper.

Much deeper.

Dusk would have fallen and still the steps continued, lamps growing few. When they paused for water, conversation had fallen away, replaced by a quiet, growing tension.

But the bottom of the flight finally did appear, revealing a mighty door illuminated by twin lamps, one low enough to flicker almost desperately.

The oak stood ajar.

As thick as Never's fingertip to elbow, the door would take a serious amount of strength to break through. That, or a little crimson-fire, but the cult had seen fit to spare him doing so. "They certainly want me here," he said as he stepped inside.

A wide chamber with a door of stone waited beyond.

The walls had changed. Now the stonework was cut as though by a mason. Had the passage above been dug to locate the chamber? Whoever had built the underground room, almost a hall, had taken care to include a diamond-like pattern; it ran horizontally along the walls, surrounded by otherwise rectangular shapes.

The door had a large crest above the steel handle; two hands wrapped around the hilt of a long sword, the outline of a sunrise behind. Or maybe it was a sunset; after all, the place was sunken beneath the mountain.

No-one recognised it, and the door did not budge.

"So this may or may not be an entrance to the Burnished King's temple then," Lakiva said.

"No record describes his crest," Sacha replied.

Never pointed to the ground before the door. Scratch and scuff marks aplenty – many of them new. "This is used frequently enough in any event."

"What is this place?" Lakiva asked. "If they tunnelled down to reach it, did they know what they were searching for? Or, was it luck?"

Never glanced around the room. The pattern and the door were the most salient features. "Perhaps it once housed furniture that would have revealed a clue," Never said. "Why does it matter? Do you sense something?"

"No... I feel like I should." He shook his head. "It doesn't make sense."

"Keep a hold of that feeling," Never said. "It might be important. And in the meantime..." He squeezed some blood from his fingertip and let the crimson-fire free; an effortless release. Then he lifted his hand and pointed at the door.

"Wait." Sacha caught his shoulder. "It will alert them."

"They know we're here and we have no key," he replied.

She frowned. "Fine. But we need to be ready for whatever lies on the other side."

"We will be." Never unleashed a torrent of fiery blood and kept the stream focused on the door. The crest began to melt, slowly sliding down the stone to land in something more puddle than anything else, and then the handle, followed by the stone, which began to turn red and then white.

Heat poured forth, casting a glow across the chamber, but Never did not stop until a hole appeared. A little longer – and then stone burst free, spinning off into the dark beyond. They pieces shot away like glowing stars, bouncing against more stone.

Once the opening was large enough to pass, he let the crimson-fire die away.

Then he groaned. "Another one."

Outbuildings of a much larger structure of stone waited – like the beginning of an underground city or, at least, a palace. Or temple.

"What is it?" Sacha asked, still blinking against the light.

"I just don't have many fond memories when it comes to underground cities, that's all."

Chapter 28.

Fragments of white-hot stone still lit the area – a cavern that stretched high into pitch darkness. It was wide, too, though more like a town than a city, based on the distance of twin pillars of moonlight that shot down from the roof across the cavern. Did they fall near an exit?

The nearby building did appear to be a temple... or at least, something grand. The diamond pattern continued within the walls, though it had grown more complex. Three storeys tall at least. The crest of the sword and sun was arranged within the diamond, looming above what appeared to be a stable – long since empty.

"Ready?" Never asked his companions. Nods; expressions of determination. "Let's follow the blood."

Spots had continued forward, crossing the stable yard. He strode after it, stepping around a hunk of red stone, and then pressed himself up against the wall of the grand building. Was the token toward stealth pointless? Anyone in the underground town knew they were inside... but why blunder around every corner?

He peered inside.

Lamps hung from the walls of the temple and ran down a long stairway into the town, casting enough light to see other buildings – homes and shops perhaps. Nothing that seemed like an inn from his vantage point, but there were two squares with a well each and what appeared to be an L-shaped barracks at the very limits of the light. From there, sparks of light seemed to lie behind the windows and the longer he stared, the more hints of movement he detected. Several large shapes, moving slowly.

"We need to know what's in those barracks," Sacha said.

"What of the temple?" Lakiva asked.

"If they are waiting for us to enter, we'll be playing into their hands but I don't want to leave a possible enemy position behind either," Sacha replied.

Never nodded. "Wait here, I'll try and find a window."

He spread his wings and leapt up, beating hard to gain height in such a still environment. When he swung around, it was to face a giant window of circular design, lit only dimly from below. Once again, the sword in the grip of hands before half a sun appeared. Few clues as to the colour of the stained glass, though it could have been red or black.

More concerning was the way it evoked the building that housed the Tree of Knowledge...

He flew closer, landing on the edge of the window, and stared within. No clues as to what waited inside. "Fine." He pushed off from the wall and twisted around to the far side of the temple where a series of tiled rooves revealed what seemed to be living quarters.

Again, no light.

He flew back to Sacha and Lakiva, landing with a shake of his head. "It's too dark. Either this is the actual trap or it's empty."

Sacha looked to Father Lakiva. "What does your Echo say?"

"There are people in the barracks but I cannot be sure how many – perhaps a hundred. The temple, I cannot say. It is not clear, as though something interferes."

"Cultists or prisoners, I wonder," Sacha replied.

"Let's rule out the temple first," Never said. "I don't think we should stay in one place for too long."

"Agreed."

Never led them into the light and then the front of the building. Twin doors, quite tall, and bearing the now familiar crest – but instead a faded engraving of a full sun, this one seemed to blaze. An odd symbol for an underground temple.

He pushed on the doors and they both swung open; one hinge screeching.

"Gods, be quiet," he told it.

The stone floor was empty beyond. No-one came charging forth and when Lakiva raised his lantern it revealed only rows of stools in rusted steel. Before each stool a small, silvery podium. These were unmarred by time and all featured curved indentations... as if for something to rest upon it? A ball? No time for a close examination. Never strode forward, stepping lightly in the emptiness as he approached the rear of the building.

A large marble statue of a soldier holding a greatsword in both gauntleted hands stood in an alcove behind a long altar, the figure's helm sat beneath one foot and the man's face was triumphant, a fierceness not lost within the marble.

Like the podiums beyond, a round hollow sat within the centre of his chest, perhaps a little bigger than a heart might have been. And it did seem that *something* had been removed. The altar below was similar, in that a mighty hollow rested in the middle of the long stone bench – it too, semi-circular. Only this was large enough that Never could have lain within and reached up to touch one side.

"What would have been here?" Lakiva asked. His expression was one of distaste. Too like his own cathedrals or too different? While it remained militaristic, it was certainly unlike any house of the Vadiya God Never had seen.

"Something of great importance... or power," Never said. The slightest remnants of what it had been, like a decaying echo, hung about the hall of worship but he could not grasp it. Yet the very fact that he had sensed something... another sign the Amouni had been involved in some manner, surely.

"Let me check the living quarters and then I think we need to pay a visit to the barracks," he said.

"Be quick," Sacha replied.

"Of course." He slipped toward a doorway. The dark corridor was empty but the next door – the one leading to the rooms beyond, was invisible in the black. He reached out and found the handle, pushing the door open but pausing after, just in case, then exiting to find a row of homes – more like huts, their narrow shapes lit from one side.

He paused – a waste of time.

The barracks held the trap; it was past time to spring it.

Never returned to the temple's main hall and found

Sacha and Lakiva waiting in silence. "Nothing," he said, and as a small group they started toward the light beyond the open doors.

His muscles grew tense as they walked. The searching was over, time was running out on the midnight deadline and whatever Dromanev had lying in wait for them, had to be stopped.

Outside, the lights beckoned, drawing them down into the town itself. While every other lamp had died or was struggling to stay alight, there was more than enough to reach level ground and lead them toward the barracks. The homes cast long shadows, all empty, few with missing glass or doors. The town had been well-preserved.

The occasional spots of blood had returned too.

Again, he followed them through the empty town, eyes roving the shadows between buildings. And finally the barracks came into view, high walls and an open gate, broad courtyard beyond. Now, unlike before, no movement. The sharp points of light still lurked within the buildings but they did not illuminate anything, just empty walls beyond the glass.

"I assume that once we enter, the trap will fall," Never said. "Check your crossbows. And ready the masks."

"We're ready," Sacha said, her face already half-covered by the kerchief.

Never pulled his own over his mouth, the damp scent of the fabric strong. He drew a blade next and pierced his skin once more, before starting forward, weapon raised, a finger resting upon the trigger as he passed through the gates and started forward.

A figure leapt down from the roof before he'd taken half

a dozen steps.

It raised a hand. "Halt, Amouni."

Human voice.

And somewhat familiar... the man from the bridge who'd first taken Temilo captive?

Never kept half his gaze upon the surrounding buildings. "Are we to deal with underlings now? Or didn't Dromanev survive my little greeting back on the Tsagadek?"

A hiss. "Do you not value the boy's life?"

"I know you would not kill someone with such a rare ability, nor would you risk turning him into a stakolin."

"No matter – you are here now; you can hear our offer. An exchange, Amouni. Your blood for his, and who knows? We may not even need it all."

Chapter 29.

Never shook his head. "Bring him here and then we'll talk."

"I have made my offer."

"Then here is my answer." Never raised his arm. Crimson-fire shot forth, throwing wild shadows. The stream struck the figure in the torso, a glimpse of his shocked face revealed – and then his scream cut short.

The sizzle of burning cloth and flesh filled the resulting silence.

"Bring Temilo here or bring me someone who can manage that simple task," Never roared.

Sacha caught his arm. "What are you doing?"

"Taking control of the situation."

"This is madness, Never. And you and I have unfinished business, I can't have you getting us all killed now."

Growling from the darkness. Drawing near. Approaching from either side of the barracks. But a new voice rang out. "Stand down, my brothers." The animalistic sounds ceased as a new, taller figure moved into the glow cast by Lakiva's lamp.

Dromanev.

The bearded leader appeared unharmed by his ride down the rapids of the Kraidav River and nor did he seem concerned over the death of one of his lieutenants. He appeared quite at ease, almost resplendent in his high-collared robe and coat of red – the choice obvious but no less menacing. His eyes burned with a hunger as he regarded Never, and a smile spread across his blue-tainted lips.

"A spirited response." His voice rasped.

"Where is Temilo?" Sacha demanded.

"Lady Isajan, how wonderful to see you once again. I see you have managed to hold on to your... lesser form." He raised an eyebrow. "And Father, I am honoured by your visit this night."

"I doubt that you are," Lakiva replied.

Dromanev shrugged. "Then let us come to an accord. As Yaras offered, we will trade the boy for Never. Know that this can be done simply, once you surrender, or via force. And, during such a tussle, I am sure that at least two of you will not survive."

"I will not be used to restore King Oleksan," Never replied.

The man's eyes narrowed. "Choose."

A crossbow bolt snapped. "Send your dogs," Sacha shouted.

Dromanev twisted, too fast, and the pouch flew wide. He snapped his fingers. Roars rang out within the barracks. Stakolin thundered from the shadows, bearing down on them, their blue, grotesque faces appearing further deformed in the dimness – five without Dromanev.

And all too close already.

Never flipped to point his weapon at the ground and fired. The pouch struck and exploded in a cloud of ash, stinging his eyes but he let his wings burst free and beat them, spreading the ash into the approaching creatures.

They slowed, gasping and coughing, one even toppling to the ground but did not stop their approach. Dromanev himself had fallen further back too.

Another bolt snapped and then glass smashed – had Lakiva fired, then thrown his lamp? The faint glow visible from the corner of Never's eye suggested the priest now had his holy nimbus in place but there was no time to confirm; the Stakolin were upon him.

Never dodged a lunge – the clawed hands had been grasping, not tearing. Never swung his own blow, connecting with an outstretched elbow. Bone snapped. He spun to face second creature, blasting it with a stream of crimson-fire. It howled but continued on.

Something struck him from behind.

He hit the stone with a grunt and rolled back to his feet. Between the two stakolin glimpses of Sacha darting forth with her rapier, and Lakiva fending blows with his war hammer, Never caught another hint of movement beyond – cultists?

And then the two creatures were upon him.

Never dodged another grasping hand and slipped within the stakolin's reach to drive his fist into the stomach – and there, bones crunched where bones ought not to have been. But the stakolin groaned as it stumbled back, wheezing now. At least the ash had worked; it *did* make them slower – but they were still two.

Something crashed atop him and he slammed into the paving.

Hot breath bore down on him, then something wet dripped across the back of his neck. Never thrashed but the weight was too much; his wings were bending too, his chest creaking.

"Be still," a voice managed.

Never blinked through tears of pain to the white light of Lakiva swinging mighty blows upon an opponent, Sacha flanking it. From nearby, Dromanev approached with a deep frown; his stride purposeful as he neared. "It is over, Amouni."

"No."

Twin cries rang out – Lakiva and Sacha, both tumbling across the yard. The stakolin reared up... only to fall to one knee, breathing heavily, blood flowing from a dozen wounds. And then it fell and did not move.

But Lakiva's light was fading and Sacha had not risen.

"No!"

Never let more crimson-fire burn, forcing more and more of his blood into a huge globe that crackled and hissed where it ate at the very air, letting it spread to cover him – his vision going red.

And he kept burning.

The creature began to howl yet it still would not move – Never pushed more blood, more fire, more fury until his own skin began to respond and finally the weight lifted. He rolled onto his back, cutting the flow, sucking in air. A large, flaming torch charged for the barracks. But the stakolin did not seek a door; instead, it burst through the very wall.

Only dust rose from the rubble, tinted orange as the creature continued to burn.

Never found one knee, still gasping for strength.

He glanced around. Where was – iron-like fingers encircled his neck, lifting him from his feet. Never snapped his hands around the creature's grip, digging his own fingers in. But the stakolin did not release him.

"That is enough – you have put on a fine display of defiance but now it ends," Dromanev said.

Never ground his teeth, still struggling for air, and urged more crimson-fire forth – but too little came and then it winked out as quickly as it rose, blood running down his hand. Too weak. Fool, he'd pushed too hard freeing himself from the other one.

"Now, time to descend at last. The Burnished King awaits."

Never kicked at the stakolin but his boots barely found his captor, not that they'd have had an effect.

Movement flashed.

Dromanev roared. The stable tilted and then Never was free, thumping to the ground. He rolled again, gasping for air once more. Above him, two figures struggled – both stakolin. The smaller of the two had driven a claw into the side of the larger, that creature's face still somewhat recognisable as Dromanev, his heavy brows containing the same gaze and his face undamaged by random eruptions of bone.

Dromanev drove an elbow down, shattering his attacker's arm, then backhanding the stakolin away. Never blinked as his vision wavered... when he could see again, two figures had joined the seemingly traitorous stakolin; Sacha and Lakiva.

She'd levelled her crossbow at the cult leader and Lakiva's nimbus was alight once more; his hammer in hand.

Dromanev cursed, then spun to dash a few steps before launching himself into the air where he cleared the barrack walls in a single bound.

The second stakolin collapsed.

Never frowned, exhaled long and slow. It hurt to swallow but he was alive – that was a blessing. He closed his eyes a moment. His limbs were heavy, far too heavy to be made of flesh and bone; they'd been replaced with stone, surely.

Footsteps rushed over.

"He's so pale." Sacha's voice. "Never?" She shook him by the shoulder and he opened his eyes.

"How did…"

"It was Illya," Father Lakiva replied. "She followed us."

Never smiled, closing his eyes once more. That was the hint of movement he'd seen before, not a cultist. "I'm happy to hear that. Is she here?"

"She said she was going to follow Dromanev – she left before we could stop her," Lakiva said. "He was heading for the temple."

"Ah. Well, she can probably take care of herself pretty well."

"Can you stand?" Sacha asked.

He nodded. "I should be able soon enough."

"I'll find some water," Lakiva said.

"And something to eat, if you've anything," Never said.

"You're hungry?" Sacha asked, incredulity in her voice.

Never rose to a half-sitting position. "Very much so – I need to regain my strength somehow."

"And eating and drinking works? It helps you produce more blood?"

"I hope so," he said as he accepted a flask from the priest. "But let's just make sure before we follow that creature, shall we?"

Chapter 30.

A cursory glance of the barracks found them empty, though sleeping pallets and meagre possessions suggested a large amount of people had been kept there recently.

"I hope the midnight deadline is now meaningless," Lakiva said as Never led them up the stairs, moving a little slower than usual. He had devoured as much food as he dared, water too, and it *had* made a difference. And while he had not pushed himself so far as on the Stair of the Wind with Snow, this time there was no chance to benefit from his brother's blood.

Still, he could fly if needed. He could fight, he could run – summoning a swathe of crimson-fire, however, was out of the question.

"It has to be," Sacha said. Her knuckles where white where she gripped her crossbow, one of only two remaining pouches of ash loaded. Lakiva had the other. The priest limped a little but did not complain. "Never was right – they wouldn't give up someone like Temilo. The truth is too valuable, it was always a lure."

"And now both Illya and I are here," Never said as they reached the halfway point.

"Which means nothing if they're all dead," Sacha replied.

"I agree."

"I am not so sure," Lakiva said. "Dead bodies will not speak of why or how this cult came to be."

Sacha glanced at the priest. "You're right but I don't want to have to choose between information and our lives – Illya can read the dead if it comes to that."

The temple loomed before them now, the doors wide open – one bearing a gouge as though a large, clawed hand had battered it agape.

Inside, nothing.

Never lifted his voice. "Illya?" No answer. Where was she now? "There must be something more to this place. A hidden passage or door," he continued.

"I can better discern the Echo now," Lakiva said. "Dromanev is beneath us; he is stronger than that which blocks me."

"Let's try the statue first," Never said.

Lakiva let his nimbus light the way as they approached the altar – where there was no need to check the statue, for a hidden stair awaited them. It descended toward a red glow.

And the faint hum of voices climbed up with the light, the words indistinct.

But it was clear that the voices were many... chanting as one.

Never glanced to Sacha who shrugged. "They're all human except for one."

"And if that's two-score voices instead of a dozen?"

"We deal with that when we get down there."

Never grinned; her answer was no doubt exactly the kind of one he usually gave people. "Down we go then."

The stairs descended perhaps two storeys, stone cut in regular form, diamonds featuring once again, but nearer the bottom, as the chanting grew in volume, something changed. The walls became pitted and when he reached out to touch them a faint dust was left behind on his fingers – and more, the wall had almost seemed to give a little under the pressure of his touch.

"Listen," Lakiva said.

Below, the chanting had dropped to a whisper. Expectant. Never frowned – a flair for the dramatic? Whatever it was, Dromanev knew they were near.

And still no sign of Illya.

Heat rose as they drew nearer the light and then the steps ended, depositing him in a narrow passage. It led to a large chamber filled with scores of kneeling men and women wearing either red robes or, far more often, rags. Red braziers kept the stone chamber warm. The walls themselves seemed almost to pulse with the light, just as seemingly decayed as in the stair – a faint scent came with it... mould?

And at the end of the chamber, a hulking figure in a loincloth with blue skin.

Dromanev.

His body was more irregular than his face – more jutting bones – but again, not so much as with the other stakolin. Was it the medicine the man supposedly took that not only allowed him to switch between man and creature but also manage the deforming effects of the *disrytha*?

The cult leader stood before a tall door of sealed stone,

unfamiliar markings climbing up its centre, runes carved like sparse, one-sided trees. The man's arms were folded across his barrel-like chest and he smiled.

"Welcome, Amouni," Dromanev called.

The chanted whisper swelled to an even speaking register, not yet too loud. The words were not modern Vadiya.

Most expressions of the prisoners remained dull. While some few faces bore darting eyes, it seemed none could flee, whether due to fear bought on by nearness of the robed Svikamet or by Dromanev or something else.

"A large audience for your death," Never shouted back.

"No. For my triumph." He gestured behind his large frame – and a much shorter figure stepped into the light. Temilo, a grim expression set upon his face. "Come, make the trade and I will set this boy free, allow your friends to take him above ground."

"We cannot trust him," Sacha said.

"I know. But I don't see another choice right now."

"I'll think of something. Just get a hold of Temilo."

Never started up the space between the cult members – who seemed only a third of the hundred or so people within the room and approached Dromanev at a stride. The man wanted Amouni blood but for what exactly? If the Burnished King lay beyond the door and the stone was sealed by Amouni hands then a mere drop of blood would be enough.

What was the rest for? Was it truly to restore the dead king? Without Illya, wasn't that impossible... unless the cult leader already had her too. But where? There was no-one else on the dais before the door. Never met Temilo's eyes and gave the boy a nod.

Temilo glanced to crowd and then back to Never, then back to the chanting fools... and those they had captured. Why? Was that where Illya was being held? Yet she was not one of the figures there. Never kept walking. Once Temilo was safe, Dromanev had to be dealt with. Which left only thirty-odd cultists to take care of. Ideally, all without hurting the prisoners.

Sacha needed to come up with something impressive.

And she wasn't the only one.

Never stopped before Dromanev. "Hand Temilo over and I will open the door."

"And everything after," Dromanev said. He gave Temilo a shove and the boy stumbled forward. Never caught him, smiling at the lad, whose expression seemed to be one of surprise. "Go to Sacha," Never said.

Temilo nodded. "Someone else is in the crowd, be careful," he said.

"I will."

Temilo ran for Sacha and Lakiva at the exit – which was now blocked by more cultists holding drawn weapons, though none made a menacing step. These men and women, however, were not entranced by their own chanting.

Never straightened with a frown. He approached the door and glanced at Dromanev, who merely stood expectantly, and lifted a hand, still mostly caked in dried blood. Never pressed it against the surface. Rumbling followed and the door slid open, revealing steps leading up into darkness.

"And the next door too," Dromanev said.

"And that is your final requirement for allowing us to leave?"

"Yes."

"If the Burnished King is there, he will unleash naught but death and destruction."

Dromanev smiled. "Assuredly."

"That is your goal? To remain after that, to become lord of nothing – vassal to his will?"

"Amouni, I am already such."

"Without a *nekromant*, you will fail."

"Is that so?" Dromanev said with a faint smile.

Never grinned, baring teeth. If he had to open another door, and if somehow something worse waited beyond, he would let Dromanev kill or be killed by it and then, kill the survivor himself. Whatever he attempted, he'd have to finish it in time to help Sacha and Lakiva. A tall order. "Then let's get you and he acquainted as quickly as possible then."

"Please."

Never started up the stair. It stretched before him, long and dark, but it did have a shaft of light at its end. Had dawn come already? He quickened his step and eventually reached the top, a circular chamber with an open roof – the cold streaming down, air sharp against his exposed skin now that he had, after a fashion, left the underground.

Within the stone chamber, merely two dozen feet across, stood only two things of note – another door, twin to that below with its lopsided, tree-like runes. A few large slabs of stone, broken and uneven, lay around it – the walls had crumbled away in places, over the centuries.

The second thing was a wide silver bowl that rested on a pedestal nearby, not unlike a bird feeder.

Never approached the bowl, moving around it to grip the sides and stare across at Dromanev, had been forced to stoop to fit his large frame within. The man's blue skin bore an unpleasant, almost grey tint in the pale light but his expression was alight with a dark joy.

"And now you must truly fulfil your end of the bargain," the creature said. "Fill that bowl with your blood."

"How do you know that?" Never demanded. "How do you know *Amouni* blood is required to open the doors, to restore your plague king?"

"That is nothing I need share with you," he said. "Now, empty your veins or must I do so for you?"

Never chuckled. "Then you've called off your vassals? Sacha is even now leading Lakiva and Temilo out of your den?"

The stakolin gave a shrug. "If that helps you with what is to come, you may believe it is so."

"Of course." Never drew a pair of knives and leapt upon the bowl, then launched himself across the chamber.

Dromanev side-stepped.

Never landed in a roll and the rush of air from a swipe of claws stirred his clothing. The moment he reached his feet he leapt forward again, charging the wall. He jumped at the stone, kicking off and up into a somersault.

Stone shattered beneath Never as his wings snapped free.

Below, Dromanev's body had penetrated the stone. The stakolin was struggling to break free, snarling as his muscles bulged. Never dove, fist raised as he bore down on the creature's head.

He swung with his birch hand – and cracked stone.

Dromanev was already free.

A clawed hand encircled the back of Never's neck and

he was twisted around to face the bowl. Never swung his knife, stabbing backward but his blade met nothing but air. He retracted his wings as best he could and dropped his weapons to grip and tear at the large fingers but only his strong hand made any progress in dragging one finger free – only for something sharp to slice into his side.

Blood flowed, pouring down his waist and legs to drip into the bowl.

"Struggle if you wish but it is pointless."

Never summoned crimson-fire... and the orange flame flickered and died. He thrashed, beating at the wrist that held him. More blood flowed. Dromanev's laughter rung in his ears.

"Never!"

A new voice – not Lakiva or Sacha.

Dromanev spun.

The pale figure of Illya stood within the rubble beside the doorway, her eyes blazing blue. She raised both hands to point at Dromanev.

"Come, creature."

"What an impressive mistake you have made – I do not need you *nekromant* but I must say; this will be easier now."

"Flee!" Never shouted but the room spun. He slammed into stone, crying out as he tumbled to the ground. He clutched his head, blood running between his fingers, pain racing through his body. The taste of iron filled his mouth.

Across the chamber, Dromanev had borne down on Illya – he swung a mighty blow.

Never opened his mouth to shout but choked on blood.

The stakolin's fist passed through her.

And then Illya's shape wavered and disappeared, leaving

the hulking brute spitting and cursing. "You are next, ghost," he roared. He turned back to Never. "But first, there is a bowl to fill."

Something other than pain coursed through his body – heat. Never frowned, he had no more strength for crimson-fire, what was it? The centre of the fire seemed to be his chest... fool! The gift!

Dromanev loomed over him. "Ready?"

Never tore the necklace free and the Fires of Heaven burst forth in a roaring bolt of green light and heat. Dromanev flew back without even a sound – thumping to the stone and lying still. Steam rose from his form.

Was it enough?

"Illya?" Never climbed to his feet, first steps unsteady. The bleeding was already slowing, but the bruising and perhaps even a crack in one of his ribs, neither were in a hurry to heal.

The stakolin had not moved and when Never stood over it, the giant hole in its chest was clear enough, even without the body's sightless eyes. Never gave the corpse a kick – and winced at the pain it caused him. "Idiot."

Chapter 31.

Footsteps echoed from the stair.

Never turned and limped over with a grunt – three figures, lit from behind by the red glow. Sacha, Lakiva and Illya too. And they moved swiftly enough. Good. Not only had they survived the cultists, they were seemingly unharmed.

Yet how had Illya appeared as a shadow of herself? More *nekromant* powers… just what else was she capable of?

Either way, he owed her his life.

"Dromanev is dead," Never said as they neared. "Thanks to Illya."

He moved back to give them room to enter. Sacha was first in and she went to him, a flicker of relief passing across her face before she glanced down at Dromanev, where she gave a nod of satisfaction. Then, she looked to the door.

"Still sealed," Never replied.

"Good."

"What about the cult members?"

"Illya dealt with most of them," Father Lakiva said. He still carried his hammer but no nimbus; and it seemed he'd not spoken before due to being somewhat winded. And why not? It had been a long night. "She took control of another stakolin – which, as soon as she impaled one of the cultists, cleared the chamber."

"More than a few have escaped," Sacha said. "There are passages and rooms we haven't explored."

"And the prisoners?"

"We have them gathering food, weapons and any other supplies. We will lead them out once we've cleansed this place," Lakiva said.

"Then before we do that, I want to be certain of something," Never said. "Somehow, Dromanev knew that Amouni blood would open this door – but the safeguard is not unlike an Amouni ruin I have seen." He shuffled closer to the door. "Guide?"

A figured robed in black blinked into view.

Like the others, it seemed as though it had been... repaired, as a slice cut through the robe and bare arm, and now the two 'halves' of the Guide were only the barest margin from being one again.

Master. This guide wore a lion's head but the voice was just as impassive as the others.

"What lies beyond this seal?"

That which cannot be released.

"The Burnished King?"

Yes. Sometimes called the Shadow of Arkenon.

"Arkenon?"

God of the Malecaphera, Master.

Never glanced to the others, but no-one seemed to recognise any of the names. "Why did I seal the King within?"

His power threatened all lands, all people. Even you, Master.
"What power?"
Plague, Drought, Famine, Death – among other Trials as faced by the Ascended.

Something that needed to stay sealed away indeed. "Can the door be opened?"

Yes. The Guide flickered but remained in place. *But it shall not be; that is the agreed upon Law.*

"Could I break the Law?"

Yes, Master. At the price of your blood, or that of another Ascended.

"Have any passed through the Seals?"

Only the lower, Master.

"And when did I last come here?"

The Guide did not answer at once. *Several seasons back now – the Verjalt month.*

Then Snow *had* been here – but had not broken the seal... which meant that even Snow, in his desire to re-shape the world, had not been willing to pass beyond the doors. "What did I seek?"

The answers to the questions you ask now.

"Did I ask why the Burnished King had been sealed but not destroyed?"

Yes.

"Tell me again," Never said.

You told us that the Shadow cannot be simply destroyed and that you could not risk removing something so vital to existence.

Never frowned but he had one more question. "Who did I have with me when we last spoke?"

One other. A human male.

"Thank you, Guide," he said. "Now, once I leave, I

command you: speak to none but I, understood?"

Yes, Master, that is understood.

"Leave us for now."

The Guide disappeared. Never let out a long sigh as he stared at the Amouni doors, their seal intact. And so it would stay, since his blood had not come anywhere near close to filling the bowl. Thankfully.

"You think Snow came here, don't you?" Sacha said.

"Yes. I also think he was repairing the Guides," Never replied. "But that's not relevant to our task here, I suppose. Of more concern; I think he brought Dromanev with him."

"Don't blame him for any of this," she snapped.

"Did I?"

"You don't have to, Never. It's clear. You think Snow exposed Dromanev to such knowledge and probably the secrets of the *disrytha* too."

He shrugged. "If he did, that hardly matters now, does it? Let's save your people."

Sacha did not answer but started back toward the stair. "Help me, Father," she said, and Lakiva glanced between them before following. Illya didn't move, however.

"I can ask Dromanev, if you wish?" she said.

Never paused. Would it make much difference? Probably not – the Guide had all but confirmed it and there seemed no need to put Illya through such a trial. While she had been pale as long as he'd know her, she appeared exhausted now. Frail instead of fleet. She had already raised who knew how many stakolin in a short space of time. "No, only if we need help dismantling what he has created."

She nodded. "The Birthing Chamber."

"You've seen it?"

"Yes – the other creatures told me. It adjoins the chamber below; I don't believe you will have too much trouble destroying it."

"Good, let's make a start then," he said, and moved to the stairs.

At first, each step sent a jolt of pain surging out from his rib but by the bottom of the flight his healing was finally underway, though he was sweating heavily, not helped by the still-warm chamber.

The red glow from the braziers stained the walls but now it also tinted the dead, darkening the Svikamet robes and the blood. Two stakolin bodies lay strewn about too but they were also joined by a few prisoners in their torn clothing.

"I could not save them all," Illya said. "Some of the cultists went for the people instead of the stakolin."

"You did more than I could have managed," Never said. Maybe if he'd been able to stop Dromanev quickly...

Pale light moved from a half-concealed entryway.

Within, an antechamber arranged with unreadable, broken-seeming runes and red drapery. A now torn curtain revealed the light; Lakiva's nimbus. Sacha moved around the adjoining room.

"This is the chamber then?" Never asked as he entered, Illya beside him.

The centre was dominated by a long silver table – not unlike the one found in Hanik's Preparation Chamber. More evidence that Oleksan had befouled an Amouni place for his temple.

Yet other than that, the place seemed... simple. A water barrel, a bench at the rear of the chamber where a mortar and pestle sat, stained red and black, and a set of chains beneath the table.

"Their store of seed must be somewhere else," Sacha said.

He nodded. "Let me melt this table down. I'll do the same to any seeds when we find them."

They left the room and he lifted the fire-stones; pointing them at the table. Heat built in his hand and he urged it forth. A funnel of green fire roared as it splashed against the table. He kept it raging until a silver pool remained – then swung the pendant to the mortar and pestle too.

When he was done, he lifted the stones to examine their still warm shape, a faint glow clear within.

"A powerful burden," he said softly.

Chapter 32.

More light entered the cavern from the distant side as morning neared noon, adding to what the rows of street lights offered. It made the movement over in the barracks easier to trace, and for the most part everything seemed fairly ordered. Someone amongst the prisoners had the right idea.

"What's the plan now?" Never asked where they stood on the steps before the temple. He blinked as his vision blurred a moment. His own weariness was catching up to him.

"Lead them back up the tunnel to the camp. Then, come back and collapse the entries and exits," Sacha said.

He nodded. "I'll handle the shaft leading to the final door."

"Good."

She began the descent. Never followed more slowly. It would have been easier to glide down, but his wings probably needed as much time to heal as the rest of him. But he didn't make them wait too long at the bottom, and by the time they reached the barracks it seemed most of the work had been done.

Groups of former prisoners, mostly fully clothed now, had gathered together around small piles, usually blankets, food or weapons. Others sat, still tying boots on and yet more simply stared into the distance, young or old, relief only a faint suggestion – it seemed, for now at least, horror was still winning out.

Those who had taken red robes had torn the sleeves free, perhaps to differentiate themselves from any remaining cult members.

At the far end of the barracks, a pile of bodies had been arranged – perhaps a dozen or more cult members – and the prisoners were discussing how best to ignite the corpses.

A tall Marlosa woman, her hair matted with blood, approached Sacha with a smile. "Lady, we are almost ready."

"I'm glad, Jeni. Have there been any attacks?"

She shook her head. "No. I have Pekev and some of the others searching."

Sacha nodded. "Send someone to bring them here – we'll leave by a stair near the temple."

"Some of them fled via the river entrance," Jeni said, glancing toward the light that fell from the roof. Her expression was one of smouldering anger.

"We will collapse that too," Sacha assured her. "But before we leave, who might know where the red seeds were stored?"

"Algodev was allowed to help them harvest the plants, he might know."

Never frowned at the way her voice had become somewhat distant. Even the torches were growing dim.

"Can you find him? We need to destroy any trace of the seed."

"Of course, My Lady."

Never blinked at a swift darkness, opening his mouth to speak, but his knees buckled. He fell but it did not seem that he hit the stones.

***

Never woke to the sounds of the camp, rustling, soft speaking, the crackle of fire and the bubbling of pots. The voices were mostly raised in laughter or cheer, and from across the camp it seemed someone was singing a victory song, his voice really rather impressive.

"Well." Someone had obviously carried him back to the camp. He'd collapsed from the overuse of crimson-fire, it seemed – yet now his limbs responded instantly, his vision was sharp.

He rose, pushing a host of blankets aside. His stomach growled as he moved – when was the last time he'd eaten? Days… weeks, surely. He rose and dressed, noting that some of the nicks and tears in his cloak had been repaired, then entered the camp.

A cheer from a nearby cook fire rose. Both soldiers and prisoners alike, all smiling over their meals. One woman waved as she approached – Moki. "Lord Never, I was so happy to hear that my little adjustments were useful to you all."

"Very much so."

"If you have the time later, I'd love to see how you were able to use the powder with your wings." She hesitated.

"Father Lakiva told me, you see."

He chuckled. "If you don't mind waiting."

"Not at all – there are still a few stakolin out there and we need every advantage we can get."

"I understand." Never thanked her again moved deeper within, pausing when he caught sight of Father Lakiva. The man stood before a sword that had been thrust into the ground, his eyes closed, hands at his sides, lips moving silently.

"Father?"

Lakiva opened his eyes and turned. He smiled when he saw who had interrupted. "Never, I am glad to see you well."

"I'm glad to *be* well," he said. "I didn't realise I had pushed myself to the very limit."

"You've been asleep for days already. I have prayed for you, even though you are not of the true faith."

"Very kind, Father. Are Temilo and Illya well also?"

"Yes. I believe Temilo is with Sacha in the command tent... Illya is resting in her cabin."

He nodded. "So, what will you do now?"

"I will send word to High Priest Firalod, requesting that my remit be extended to further study what occurred here."

And no doubt, to study Illya. "Let me know if I can help," Never said. "And thank you, Lakiva. We couldn't have put a stop to Dromanev without you."

"You flatter me."

Never slapped him on the shoulder and started for the command tent, weaving through the tent lines but a voice stopped him.

"Never."

Sacha sat upon a large crate of armour between two

tents, straw peeking from beneath the lid. Her expression was almost dull... emotionless, but her voice had been firm. Her armour gleamed and her red cloak covered her hands, though beneath she no doubt carried a blade.

"This is truly what you seek?" he asked.

She nodded as she hopped down. "Follow me."

Sacha led him from the camp and along the road a little, turning to trudge through the snow before the trees. He followed in the holes made by her boots. "The prisoners are well?" he asked.

"Yes."

Within the trees the noon sun was weaker, barely penetrating to reach the thin path but ahead, a bright clearing.

"And you were able to destroy the seeds?"

"Yes."

She pushed a branch aside, scattering snow as she did. He paused, letting it settle before repeating her action and stepping into the clearing. Here, the snow had mostly melted away, leaving the cold, stony earth ringed by white and the black of the pines in turn. The footing below was not slick and it was even enough; a fair place for a fight to the death.

If one combatant wasn't Amouni.

And he would not kill her.

"I let you sleep for days, so I assume you are ready?" She threw her cloak back and drew her blade – she'd switched back to her longsword now.

"For this? No." He drew a pair of daggers and let his wings free.

A black feather twisted down to the earth.

"Do not insult me, Never."

"My reluctance is an insult?"

She pointed at him with a gauntleted hand. "Yes, God be damned, yes!"

Never hurled one of his daggers – aiming for her leg. She leapt aside. The blade clattered across the ground. "Exactly like that," she shouted. "Aim to kill, you coward!"

She leapt forward, slashing pattern from high to low, pivoting to anticipate his evasion. But he kept his distance, wings aiding him. Had she grown faster? Her moves were swifter; he caught a blow on one blade, deflecting it. But it cost him a weapon, the dagger knocked free.

He leapt into the air, beating his wings as he drew another knife.

She spun away to create space.

Never swung around to slash at her, again, aiming to wound – but she ducked aside. And once more, she was too fast. She was the far superior warrior when it came to the blade but her speed was now something unnatural.

Sacha had been changed by his blood after all.

He attacked again, slashing low and seeking to get within her reach, so he could strike a blow with his fist, something that would injure, and not draw blood… but she was too swift. Her own blade flicked out and nicked his wrist and then his cheek when he twisted away.

Never threw himself back, gliding to a halt as he landed across the clearing.

Breath steamed, both the air from his mouth and that from hers – she was breathing harder than he; she'd been fighting in a real duel. He had not.

She charged.

Never leapt into the air and bore down on her once more. This time, she drew her blade back and lunged, jabbing upwards. He rolled aside but did not pull up, and it seemed, caught her off-guard – since she did not move to avoid him.

He crashed into her.

They slid across the stone, her breastplate screeching, and came to a halt at the edge of the clearing in a spray of snowflakes. Sacha struggled but he caught her sword arm with his birch hand, pinning her with the rest of his body weight. "Why demand this?" he hissed.

"You are not so clueless, Never. You should understand." Her jaw was clenched. "Kill me or be killed."

"No!" Never snapped. "Those aren't the only options here."

"They are for me."

He leant closer, his own anger rising – though it was borne more of frustration than rage. "All this because he chose me instead of you? Is that what it is?"

Her eyes widened and her mouth fell open.

Never flinched at her expression; it was such a raw pain, like nothing he'd ever seen on her face. She'd always been so strong, Gods, she had not once let herself be so vulnerable and now… now it was though he'd driven a dagger into her with his cruelty.

But the shock did not last.

She thrashed beneath him with a snarl but he did not move. "I cannot change what he did," Never said, speaking softly now.

Sacha was trembling.

"He could have killed me so many times but… in the end, he was my brother again – not the monster I thought he became."

Tears built in her eyes. "You would not call him that if you truly understood."

He kept speaking. "I understand. He saved me. He sacrificed his life, his dreams, his vision of the future – do you think he would want me to kill you to save myself? Or that he would want you to kill me?"

Sacha thrashed again, harder, but he held her in place somehow. She screamed. "I told you, you don't understand. It's not just his death, Never. Being around you is pain! You're like him, your sense of power, your face by God – and mixed in with it all are my memories of you. You are my past but he was my future. Every moment is a reminder of what I have lost, can't you see that?"

"Then take a new future," Never said. "People rely on you here. You matter to them – why did we risk our lives for Temilo if you were just going to do this right after we saved him?"

She shook her head but she stopped fighting him – though he did not let her go yet. "Why can't you admit it?"

"Admit what?"

"That you're not the only one who lost a loved one."

"I..." He stumbled for words. "Sacha... I... you think I don't realise you have suffered too?"

She gasped, hissing a word that was unintelligible.

He waited.

"Maybe... Maybe if you'd been able to say it then..." She closed her eyes, tension flowing from her limbs. "Let me up, Never." He moved aside and she rose into a sitting position. She met his gaze and the fierceness had returned to her blue eyes. "I had imagined this moment... but not like this."

"I'm sorry," he said. "You're right – I can't understand

what you've lost."

She swallowed, and broke into what was a cross between a sob and laughter. "Now you say it, you blasted fool."

He stood, then extended her hand. She took it and he helped her up. "And will you live now?"

"I hadn't meant to die, Never."

He grinned. "Maybe you'd have beaten me if you'd taken a little more of my blood – it changed you, you know."

She nodded. "Yes. I feel faster. And stronger."

"I hope that it is only a gift."

She reached up and placed a hand on his cheek, her hand cool. "You still think it's a curse, after all this time? After everything you've done – the people you've helped? Even here, those who you had every right to consider enemy?"

"Maybe not," he said with another smile. He raised his hand to take her own, giving it a squeeze before lowering it. "Goodbye, Sacha."

She nodded before stepping back, a trace of regret plain in her eyes. "Remember your promise – we've already caved in the first two entries."

"I'll deal with it right now."

Never flexed his wings once more, a slight wince for the bruising on his back, and then leapt into the air, beating his wings to break from the clearing. He glanced down as he did, Sacha stood motionless, watching him.

Chapter 33.

A chill entirely beyond the wind enveloped him as he crouched by the opening of the shaft that descended to the final Seal – great rents and cracks in the stone, twin impressions near his boots. He did not touch them, for it seemed, like in the temple below, that the rock had somehow become... diseased, as though it were decaying without turning to dust.

Similar gouges led down the walls.

Or, in this case – *up*.

For no-one could reach his precarious position without wings; the climb would have been too difficult, and thus no-one had climbed down into the shaft.

But something had climbed out.

He stood and turned to take in the white peaks surrounding him. Clouds drew near, grey and mute – though further in the distance, the threat of lightning and rain. Whatever had left was long gone. Sacha had let him sleep for days. And those who'd been tasked with collapsing tunnels or entryways below, would not have noticed anything occurring above.

And thus, they had survived.

Never sliced into his palms, replaced his blade then stepped into the shaft – locking his wings as he did.

He glided down, jaw clenched.

Blood pooled gently.

How.

How had the seal been broken? The guide could not have failed – the bowl had not been filled!

Before he reached the floor, he let twin globes of fire snap around his fists. One of the doors lay half open, the other still closed. A thin... mist hung in the air, as if part of a barrier that remained in place.

Two corpses lay by the silver bowl.

The silver bowl stood empty – though the insides were streaked with blood, as though it had been full before. Yet now, a small opening lay in the bottom of the bowl. Had it drained away? Was that how the blood unlocked the sealed doors?

Never knelt beside the first corpse.

Stakolin.

Long slashes up each wrist. Similar cuts to the throat and inner thigh. It had been bled dry. "By all the Gods."

The other corpse was human. Red robes, sleeves intact. Someone had obviously lain low during Illya's attack and the liberation of the prisoners. And the damnable fool had somehow used the stakolin blood to free the Burnished King... and been rewarded by losing his head, the stump of a neck rested in a pool of black blood.

Never stood. "Guide."

The lion-headed guide did not appear.

He raised his voice. "Guide, appear now. Your master calls."

Still naught but his voice bouncing off the stone. But even without the Guide to confirm his guess, well, whether it was right or wrong mattered little, truly. Perhaps the blood of the very first stakolin had been, mixed with Snow's own blood. Such was his tendency to experiment... which meant that some of Never's pure blood and a *lot* of the diluted blood from a stakolin had been enough to break or at least weaken the seal.

The proof lay before him.

Never strode forward. The mist was no barrier, he passed within as if ushered into the darkness by its touch.

He flared the crimson-fire, illuminating his surroundings.

The red and orange light revealed a small room only, large enough for a throne set against the wall. And empty throne; this also of silver but perhaps three times as large as natural for a human. Bigger even, than what would suit a stakolin.

Yet the surface had been dulled in the outline of human shape – even the arms, where hands must have rested, appeared tarnished.

There, where the Burnished King must have sat, imprisoned for centuries upon centuries.

Once the seal was broken, how was he able to escape?

Said to be the Shadow of a God, perhaps he needed little aid after all... and what had the Guide claimed? *Shadow cannot be simply destroyed.* Never spun and charged back into the shaft, where he leapt into the air and began the climb.

The shadow of an ancient plague god was loose in the world.

And if it could not *simply* be destroyed, or at least, resealed, that did not preclude the task being completed with great difficulty.

Which is exactly what he would do.

And that meant learning more about the God Arkenon.

Part of his search for answers could be undertaken in Kiymako. After all, the gift of the Great Phoenix seemed prescient now. And did he really need an excuse to visit his sister? Not truly. In any case, he would scour every story, every history and every myth in the lands, all that he could find – starting with the library hidden in the Amber Isle.

A Note from Ashley

Hello! While you wait for Never's next adventure (Throne of Leaves) I thought you might enjoy my other epic fantasy series, which begins with *City of Masks:*

A noble daughter burdened by power she never sought.

Perched on an unforgiving coast, the city of Anaskar is under threat from enemies within. Its own royal family feuds over possession of sentient bone masks of power, leaving Sofia Falco, daughter to the city's Lord Protector, to foil a conspiracy designed to strip her father of both his title and powerful Greatmask.

A bitter mercenary accused of murder.

Yet when disaster strikes, Sofia is forced to flee the palace and into the city where she crosses paths with mercenary Notch. But Notch has his own problems - accused of murder, he must fight to clear his name, all the while hunted by the city's robed assassins, the very people who are now searching for Sofia...

Follow two unlikely heroes on an epic fantasy adventure where the struggle over bone masks of powert hreatens to tear their city - and kingdom - into shreds.

Acknowledgements

Once more, a very deep appreciation to Lin Hsiang for the amazing cover (the eighth so far!) and also Vivid Covers for bringing everything together with the title design. And also but especially to my editor Amanda at Phoenix Editing!

Finally, to my loved ones - thank you too!

Thanks for reading and keep an eye out for announcements for Never's 8th adventure, Throne of Leaves.

Ashley

About Ashley

Ashley is a poet, novelist and teacher living in Australia. Aside from reading and writing, he loves volleyball, Studio Ghibli and Magnum PI, easily one of the greatest television shows ever made.

You can find him online at Twitter or on his fiction blog, City of Masks and at ashleycapes for poetry. As if that's not enough, you can also sign up to his newsletter for free books, competitions, giveaways and sneak peeks of forthcoming titles!

Also by Ashley Capes

The Fairy Wren
A Whisper of Leaves
Crossings
Somnus and the March Hare

The Bone Mask Trilogy
1. City of Masks
2. The Lost Mask
3. Greatmask

Book of Never
1. The Amber Isle
2. A Forest of Eyes
3. River God
4. The Peaks of Autumn